# The SHELL BOX

## CAROL OLDHAM

**Scripture Union**

130 City Road, London EC1V 2NJ

**For younger readers by the same author:**
The Birthday Puppy

© Carol Oldham 1989
First published 1989

ISBN 0 86201 542 1

Phototypeset by Input Typesetting Ltd, London
Printed and bound in Great Britain by Cox and Wyman
Ltd, Reading

# Contents

*For Kathryn, Anna and Julia*

# 1

## *The football match*

'It's no good!' cried Laura. 'I'm stupid, thick, useless. A walking disaster!'

'I'll agree with that,' grinned her older brother, as he closed the front door behind her and watched his sister dripping on the doormat. 'Why didn't they cancel the match with all this rain?'

'Because,' hissed Laura, her teeth chattering uncontrollably, 'It's the *tournament*, the girls' five-a-side football tournament, the day we've been waiting for all year!'

Tim watched Laura shivering there, brown-streaked legs in sodden muddy boots, shorts and T-shirt soaked, black hair clinging flatly to her head, brown eyes fighting back the tears. It was obvious her team had lost.

'Cheer up,' he said in a kindly way. 'You can try again next year.'

'You don't understand,' wailed Laura bitterly, amidst sniffs and gulps. 'I failed them. I let them down. I let in the winning goal!' She threw her goalkeepers' gloves disgustedly onto the floor. Five pounds they'd cost her dad, because she wanted new ones for the big occasion. Now she never wanted to look at them again.

'No need to eat my head off,' snapped Tim. 'I was only trying to help.' When Laura was upset, she was angry, and when Laura was angry she would hit out at anyone who came near her.

'I'm running you a bath,' called Mum from the top of the stairs. 'Come and tell me all about it.'

Laura climbed slowly and heavily towards the steamy, perfumed smell of warm bubble bath. All her hopes had been shattered. All that practising for nothing. Knocked out in the very first round. Why, oh why were they drawn to play the strongest team first? The team that went on to win the whole event. And why did she have to fall flat in the mud and make a fool of herself? Everything she touched went wrong. The captain would be furious with her. The gang would never speak to her again. They would choose someone else to take her place. Her one big chance – and she'd blown it completely!

Mum was sympathetic and gentle, 'Don't worry, dear. It's not the end of the world!' she said, rubbing hard at her daughter's short curly hair. 'Sure you haven't been swimming instead of playing football? I'll go and get you a warm drink and put dinner in the oven. You'll soon feel better. There *are* more important things in life than football, you know!'

When Dad came home he was kind too. 'Never mind,' he said, throwing her a bar of chocolate. 'I'm proud of you for taking part. Better luck next time!'

But none of them really *understood*.

And as for God, who was supposed to understand everything! Well, he'd really let her down! She'd prayed for weeks about this football match. She'd tried her hardest to be good, she'd stopped arguing about washing up, she and Tim hadn't had a proper fight for at least a week. *And* she'd put in all the effort of training, because, as Mum warned her, you could ask God to help you, but you'd still got to work.

Laura was tearful and cross as she ate her dinner. The lumps of carrot stuck in her throat, and the meat was still there after a hundred chewings.

She was angry as she did her piano practice too, the one thing she was really good at, even brilliant.

'Laura has such feeling for the music,' her teacher would say. She's very talented for one so young.' Tonight she thumped and banged the keys mercilessly, chose all her noisiest, most discordant pieces, until Mum made her stop in case poor Mrs Simkins next door got one of her migraines!

'Read a book,' suggested Dad. But Laura could never concentrate on anything other than comics, or thin books with large print and plenty of pictures.

'Watch telly,' suggested Tim, but there was nothing suitable on, and her family had not yet invested in a video, or even a stereo for that matter. James next door had a computer in his bedroom. The humming and the buzzing and the beeps and the flashing screen kept him occupied every evening. Mick, on the other side, had a new bike, so he rode round the streets all evening. And Philippa, two doors down, was out with her dad in their new boat.

And all Laura wanted – wanted *so* much – was to be popular with the 'gang' of girls of school, to be accepted, to be needed, to be important.

'I'm never going to pray again,' she whispered to herself with close determined lips, as she climbed into bed that night and lay stiffly beneath the flowered cotton quilt.

But what about the school disco? An uneasy thought made her not quite so sure of herself. She needed a new dress for the disco. And she couldn't ask Dad for one, not after the gloves. All the other girls had new dresses, all the same colours, all the latest fashion. The shop in town had done a roaring trade. And Kate was having her ears pierced, and Michelle had high heels, and Natalie was having a perm and Joanna's mum let her wear make-up. And she, Laura, as usual, would be the odd one out, with a babyish cotton skirt that was out of date years ago and her frilly blouse that Mum said looked so pretty!

Reluctantly Laura decided she needed to give God one more chance. 'If you find me the money for a new disco dress,' she prayed, 'I'll forget all about the football, and I'll be good as gold all day long. A perfect angel!'

'And one more thing, God,' she added sleepily, and somewhat sadly, as she turned out her bedside lamp, 'I really do need a new friend.'

# 2

## The disco dress

Laura awoke to a brilliant sunny morning. And the idea in her head as she flung open the bedroom window was just as brilliant!

'I'll earn the money,' she smiled, breathing in the fragrance of the morning air, and glancing down at the patio with its tubs of petunias and pansies, and her prize sunflower climbing steadily towards the sky. Seven days there were until the disco, and the disco dress cost seven pounds.

'That's a pound a day,' she calculated. 'It's going to be hard work, but I'll *do* it! Now, where to start?'

It was unnecessary to look further than the bedroom floor, for there, in a heap, were about five changes of clothes – her old faded jeans, new white shorts, a Mickey-mouse T-shirt, a grey school sweat-shirt, her green track-suit, a pink jump-suit and a crushed blue and white school dress! Laura was untidy. She had always been untidy, and now she had reached the age of ten, Mum had decided that cleaning the bedroom was her daughter's own responsibility.

Laura hurriedly and forcefully stuffed the lot into her wide bottom drawer, apart from the thick track-suit, which she flung round a too small hanger and placed in her wardrobe. She shook her duvet wildly in the air, and in so doing knocked several ornaments off the dressing-table. The head came off the pink and pretty china model of a girl, which Laura had never liked, so she dropped it happily into the waste bin. Her elephant money box she replaced with care, empty though it was. It was going to be overflowing by the end of the week!

Laura straightened her pink fluffy rug, placed her slippers under the bed and paused to see what else might be hiding there. There were three odd socks, Ah, that was where the yellow one with the black spots had got to!, some toffee papers, an apple-core, a cutting of her favourite pop group, a scribbled note saying how much she hated a girl in her class who was always bullying her, her luminous pink marker pen, a partly-chewed rubber, the missing head-phones from the personal stereo Tim had given her for her birthday, and her collection of prize marbles – moonies, small and large, milkies with varying tints of blue and yellow and green, and her beautiful black special, which she polished reverently before replacing it, wrapped in tissue, in her marble tin. No one in school had one like that.

A glance at her alarm clock told Laura it was time for breakfast. She leapt the last few stairs, kissed her mother, hugged her father and patted her brother on the shoulder as she took her place next to him at the dining-room table, to begin her breakfast.

'What's up with you?' asked Tim in amazement. 'Thought you'd still be sulking over yesterday.' Twelve year old brothers are never very tactful.

'I'm glad you're feeling better, dear,' smiled Mum.

12

'What do you want for your packed lunch today?'

'Don't worry, I'll make it myself,' announced Laura cheerfully, between mouthfuls of cereal. Dad almost dropped the milk-jug and Tim half choked on the toast he was eating.

'You feeling all right?' he queried. 'Didn't get a bang on the head in that match, did you?'

'Nope,' grinned Laura, sailing into the kitchen. 'Want me to make yours as well?'

'No fear!' said Tim emphatically. 'Not if those cakes you cooked are anything to go by!'

Laura made her ham sandwiches, filled her flask with squash and set about clearing the table.

'Thank you,' said her mother. 'You *are* in a good mood!'

There was just time to wash up, including the milk-pan, before leaving for school, and Laura even wiped over the stains on the cooker.

'Now,' she beamed at her mother, 'what d'you think that's worth?'

'Ah,' laughed Tim, 'now I know what you're after! You can clean my shoes tonight if you like!'

'Oh,' said Mum, with a mixture of amusement and disappointment, 'I thought this was too good to be true!'

'Well,' decided Dad, picking up the car keys, 'if you keep it up, perhaps you can have a rise in pocket money – at the end of the week!'

On the way to school Laura peered in through the door of the clothes shop where the girls bought their disco dresses. There were fewer on the rail than before, but still at least five, white they were, covered with coloured hearts and with red satin sashes. She was sure one of them would be hers.

After school that night she decided to visit Gran. She

13

loved her dearly and visited her regularly, because she so enjoyed seeing the pleasure on the gentle old face as Gran opened the door to her favourite grand-daughter. But that was not the only reason for calling on Gran tonight. Gran always gave her a gift as she left, usually a packet of sweets and a fifty pence piece, or, occasionally, if she'd run out of sweets, a whole pound coin! Laura very much hoped that she'd run out of sweets today!

Gran's pale blue eyes lit up and her lined but pretty face broke into smiles, as Laura joked and chatted and told all that had been happening at school and at home over the past week.

'But, Gran,' she added with a sudden frown, 'the football match just wasn't fair! The team we played were massive! They looked at least thirteen! And they were so rough! Called themselves the Hillbury Horrors!'

Gran's eyes widened and she shook her grey curls disapprovingly. 'Don't know what you want to play football for,' she muttered. 'Silly game. You could end up with a broken arm or leg.'

'Now, listen, dear,' she continued, opening the kitchen drawer and taking out a flat brown parcel. 'Today I've something special for you.' Laura's heart sank, her hopes of a pound coin were fading fast. 'It's a sewing set, tapestry you know, like I used to do when I was a girl. That'll keep you busy, take your mind off all these dangerous sports!'

Laura kissed her grandmother, and thanked her politely. She looked with dread at the mass of coloured wools and intricately printed floral canvas. 'It's mmm . . . really unusual,' she stammered. I'd be a granny myself before I stitched all that, she thought to herself! Fundraising day number one had not been a tremendous success!

Days two, three, four, five and six were not much better. Nobody wanted their windows cleaned or their dogs taken for walks or their babies looked after. And nobody was interested in buying her sketches or her painted plaster models, or the fudge she made which didn't set properly. And, worst of all, by day number six there was only one dress left on the rail!

As she walked dejectedly up the garden path, Laura had just about given up hope. So God's not interested in me after all, she thought, despite all Mum has told me, and despite all they say at church and Sunday School. She wanted that dress very badly, but, deep down, she also wanted to feel sure that God did care for her.

'Hi, sis,' greeted Tim, as he opened the door. 'Great news!' he announced, flinging his arms in the air as if he were some famous actor about to speak his most important lines. 'We are to be honoured by a visit from Great Aunt Maude!'

Laura's face fell even further. 'Oh, no,' she moaned, 'that's all I need!'

She dropped her schoolbag in the hall in her usual way.

'Put it in the cupboard,' shouted Mum above the hum of the hoover, 'and then could you flick round with the duster? I wasn't expecting visitors!'

'Aunt Maude isn't a visitor,' Tim commented dryly. 'She's an inspector!'

It was true. Wherever Aunt Maude went, if there was a chip, or a crack or a smudge, a piece of dirt anywhere, a hair out of place, she would spot it.

Mum had tried her hardest: there were fresh flowers on the polished table, the best mats, shiny cutlery, crystal glasses; books, magazines, records, tapes, board-games – all had been tidied away in one fell swoop; and the picture of herself Aunt Maude had given them last Christmas was once more on display on the mantelpiece.

A taxi drew up outside.

'Here we go,' said Tim, 'best foot forward!'

'Just be careful,' said Mum in a tense whisper, while untying her apron and hiding it in the umbrella stand, 'and for goodness' sake don't argue!'

'Laura, my dear, how you've grown!' boomed Aunt Maude, her eyes taking in every minutest detail. 'You've cut your hair, how sad! Those pigtails were much neater, more hygienic. That button's loose on your blouse. Don't lose it, dear. Odd ones look so untidy. Tim, my word, quite a young man, and much thinner than before! Help me with my bag, would you? I've a present there for each of you.'

What will it be this time, wondered Laura. An encyclopaedia of good manners, One Hundred Ways to Please an Eccentric Aunt?

'Aunt, you must be tired,' ventured Mum, helping the tall, thin, blue-haired old lady off with her expensive jacket and stepping backwards, slightly overpowered by the strong perfume with which Maude always showered herself. Great Aunt might be fussy and prim about details, but she wore very stylish clothes. Black silk suit, no less, huge crocodile-skin handbag and enough jewellery to start a shop.

Dinner was not the pleasant meal Mum hoped it would be, despite the candles. In fact the candles were the problem. Tim knocked one over, as he reached for the roast potatoes, and it, in turn, smashed into Great Aunt's glass of apple juice. At least it put out the flame!

'In my young days,' Aunt frowned disapprovingly,

16

'children offered the dishes first to their elders and betters! You two should have more respect for your parents. Tut, tut, tut, what *do* they teach you in these vulgar days?'

Then there was the problem of Laura leaving her meat untouched. 'What a waste, shameful for a growing girl,' remarked Great Aunt, at the same time delicately leaving quite a pile of food at the edge of her plate. Different rules for adults, thought Laura resignedly.

After dinner entertainment was next.

'Now show me what you've learnt since my last visit,' ordered Great Aunt, while seating herself, like a queen on a throne, at the far end of the lounge.

Laura sat down obediently on the piano stool, and her dad switched on the wall light nearby.

'Back straight,' came the order. 'You look like a floppy doll! And remember – curve those finger ends!'

With a sigh Laura began to play – Beethoven, Brahms, Schumann, Liszt – silvery notes floated out of the baby grand piano and the whole atmosphere changed. Laura loved music.

Great Aunt listened entranced. She was relieved that these somewhat common relations of hers had at least one worthwhile interest, and she actually looked as though she was enjoying it.

The silence at the end of the performance was something no-one dared to break. Except Great Aunt herself.

'*Exquisite*, my dear,' she enthused. 'The essence of perfection! Now children,' she continued, 'come and receive your presents.' She fumbled in her large black handbag for quite some time, obviously becoming more hot and bothered every moment.

'How awful!' she finally announced. 'How unforgivable! I must have left your presents at home.'

'No great loss,' muttered Tim, only to be quietly kicked by his father.

'However,' continued Great Aunt Maude, composing herself once more, 'such playing deserves reward. Laura, my dear, please accept this gift and use it to buy a book, a book on the history of classical music.'

With that she delved into her black crocodile-skin wallet and handed Laura, wonder of wonders, a crisp blue five pound note! Tim's scoffing turned to envy. With prizes like that around, he wished he had kept up his trumpet playing!

Laura grinned from ear to ear. God's done it! she thought to herself. At the last minute he's actually done it. Two pounds in my money box and five more make seven — seven pounds for my disco dress!

It was late when father drove Aunt Maude home, after a most successful visit. Laura knelt by her bed. 'Dear God,' she murmured, 'thank you, thank you, thank you so much.' And she lay down to dream of flashing lights and pounding music and herself, the most attractive girl in the whole school, in a flouncy new disco dress!

# 3

## Theresa

'Whew!' whistled Tim in admiration. 'One hip, cool, trendy kid! Can I escort you to the disco, madam?'

'No thanks,' answered Laura, brushing past him to check her appearance in the long hall mirror. 'Dad's taking me.'

A final flick of her fringe, toss of her dangly gold borrowed clip-on ear-rings, and a twirl in the famous disco dress and Laura was ready.

The Middle School Disco was really the social event of the year – as far as the older classes of the school were concerned. Nobody, but nobody, stayed away, apart from the few whose parents disapproved. At seven o'clock mums and dads were seen walking their offspring down the road, eyeing all the latest fashions, coloured hair, luminous socks, spotted ties, the more outrageous the better! Dad was rather proud of Laura. Attractive and 'with it', he thought, without going over the top.

Laura joined her classmates in a group dance in one corner of the decorated hall. For once she felt good, as good as the others, for once she felt she belonged. Laura danced all evening, stopping only once for a coke and some crisps. The beat was too inviting to miss a moment. Nine o'clock came far too quickly, however, and there was Dad at the gate once more, ready to take his bright-eyed daughter home to bed.

The last day of term was always a hectic one. Giving in books, Laura was glad to say good-bye to hers with all their blots and red ink crosses, emptying desks down to the last frilly-edged wooden pencil shaving, saying farewell to the fourth years, being told for the thousandth time to keep quiet, so that the teacher could write up her next term's register.

Laura's standing with the 'gang' was quite reasonable after the night of the disco. She was really a very pretty girl, slim and graceful — lacking only in self-confidence. Seven different boys had asked her to dance, which made her the most sought-after girl in the class, a fact that the usual leaders seemed to respect.

But still she realised that not one of them was really a friend. A friend should be someone you could trust all the time. These girls were likely to smile at your face and spread unkind rumours behind your back. They found it amusing when you felt down and giggled when you made a mistake. They laughed when you got low marks, as Laura usually did, and found it hilarious to embarrass you further by hiding your pencil case in a boy's desk, or stuffing your PE kit into the waste paper basket. Kindness was considered weakness, good behaviour they called crawling to the teacher, and Laura's biggest failing, in their eyes, was that she never swore.

There was a quieter group of girls in the class, but Laura, being a lively spark, found them boring. Since her best friend, Jayne, had moved to Scotland, there seemed no-one just like her.

Still, she thought, God had answered her prayer for a disco dress, and she felt sure that he would find her a new friend. As Mum said, these things take time. We don't always have immediate answers. We have to be patient. The most likely thing to happen, thought Laura, was that a new girl would start in September, a girl with whom she could share everything.

Laura could hardly wait till home time. She knew what she would find – Mum up to her eyes in packing suitcases, Dad checking the car and fixing on the roof rack, the kitchen smelling of baking, the hall littered with tennis rackets, beach balls, cricket stumps, wellington boots. And it would be fish and chips from the corner shop for tea! And an early night, for next morning, at crack of dawn, they would be off for two weeks' holidays in the wild and rugged mountains of Wales!

When Laura arrived home, however, it was not at all like that. The car was gone; the kitchen was tidy, no sign of flasks or coolbags or boxes of food; in the middle of the lounge was a basket of old baby toys they usually kept in the attic; and Mum was nowhere to be seen!

'Mum, where are you?' yelled Laura.

'Up here, love,' came the reply, and Laura realised the loft ladder was down. Climbing quickly, with a sense of panic, her schoolbag still on her arm, Laura peered up into the dim area under the eaves, where Mum was balancing on rafters and trying to reach something hidden in the furthest corner.

'Here it is,' she announced triumphantly, 'your old car seat!' She placed it in the middle of the loft, which was floored, together with a high-chair, a pushchair, and the cream and yellow sections of an old cot!

Laura climbed gingerly into the loft and sat down

amidst dusty cardboard boxes, Tim's old train set and a pile of blankets.

'What's going on?' she asked in bewilderment.

'There's been a change of plans,' said Mum, busily checking that all the cot screws were still there and wiping some fluff from the picture of a puppy on the far end. 'We're not going on holiday tomorrow now, we're . . .' Laura didn't give her mother a chance to finish.

'Why not?' she demanded. 'What's happened? Are Alice and Mark ill or something?' Alice and Mark were their cousins who were supposed to be joining them, the two families sharing a large house in Wales.

'No, it's all right,' replied Mum calmly. 'Mark and Alice and Auntie Pam and Uncle Barry are going tomorrow and we're joining them on Sunday.'

'But why?' persisted Laura angrily. 'Why do we have to be late? They'll pinch all the best bedrooms!'

'Because,' explained Mum, 'we have a little visitor coming. You know Dad and I have had our names down on the fostering list, for looking after children, for some time now, and you know that Mrs Samuels, the social worker, has interviewed us and everything? Well, quite suddenly, much sooner than we expected, there's a little girl who needs a home for a fortnight. Her mother's going into hospital. It's only a short-term foster — at least at the moment it is. They were desperate for somewhere to place her. I'm sure you'll love looking after her.'

Laura pursed her lips and tensed her whole body.

'You might have told me!' she fumed.

'I didn't know till this morning!'

'You could have said no, especially as we're going on holiday!'

'We didn't want to say no. We want to help this little girl.'

22

'Where's she supposed to sleep then? She's not coming in my room!'

'All right,' said Mum quietly, 'if that's the way you feel, we'll have the cot in our room!'

'When's she arriving?'

'Dad's gone to fetch her and the social worker now.'

Laura climbed down the ladder, threw her bag on her bed, and flung herself down beside it. 'What a great start to a holiday,' she whispered bitterly. 'Mark and Alice are really going to love this! How can we climb mountains with a baby?'

Mum handed down the cot and other items to Tim, who had just arrived home from school. He was as disappointed as Laura, but thought it best to keep quiet about it at the moment. He would ring up his friend and say he could go swimming this evening after all. He was an excellent long-distance swimmer.

The car turned into the driveway, Mum pulled a brush through her hair, dabbed on some lipstick and ran to open the front door, calling to the children as she did so, 'Please come and welcome her! Her name's Theresa!'

In walked Mrs Samuels, a smile on her face, and clinging tightly to her, her head buried in her shoulder, was a little Asian girl, with dark wavy hair, chubby legs and a white cotton dress on.

Mum welcomed them into the lounge and asked Tim to put the kettle on. Dad pulled out some toys, building bricks and a wobbly clown, and tried to entice Theresa out of Mrs Samuels' arms.

The frightened little two year old hung grimly onto her only friend and refused to show her face.

Laura, for all her display of quick temper, was compassionate really, and the sight of this lost little one made her eyes prick with tears. Suddenly, she felt very ashamed. There was she, moaning about postponed holiday plans, when this little girl had been uprooted from her home and family.

Another thought bothered her even more. She had promised God she would be good if he answered her prayer. Good as gold, she'd said, a perfect angel. And, in the space of one day, she'd completely forgotten all about it!

Laura wiped her eyes and glanced over at the nervous newcomer. Theresa had at last looked up from Mrs Samuels' shoulder and her eyes, enormous, dark brown and questioning, met Laura's and gazed at her steadily and suspiciously.

Laura suddenly remembered her prayer for a friend, and realised that this little girl's need was much, much greater. How could she expect God to find her a friend if she refused to be a friend to someone in need?

Mum tried to coax Theresa onto her lap, while Mrs Samuels drank her tea. She offered her a cup of milk and a biscuit. She was as gentle and loving as could be, but it made no difference. Laura hunted in the toy basket for something really special and then she remembered her best doll, the one with the red dress and long dark hair, the one she'd really outgrown, but still liked to sit on her shelf, like a pleasant memory. She ran upstairs to fetch it, and Theresa's eyes followed her as she left the room.

The doll was the turning point. Maybe it was the bright red dress, or the eyes which closed and the eyelashes which fluttered, or the cord you pulled to make her talk, but Theresa took hold of the doll when it was offered to her, and made no complaint when Mrs Samuels, on leaving, sat her down on Laura's lap!

'You *can* put the cot up in my room,' said Laura to

her mum and dad later, as they tried to persuade Theresa to eat some tea, 'and I'm sorry about all the fuss, Mum.'

It was Laura who tucked up the uncomplaining little toddler in her new bed. It was Laura who read her a story and sang her a lullaby. It was Laura who took her old night light out of the cupboard and offered to leave it on all night, and it was Laura who went to bed very early just to keep an eye on Theresa.

And it was Laura who, finding her new charge awake, silently wide-eyed and worried in the middle of the night, let down the cot side and lifted the warm child gently into her own bed and rocked her to sleep in her comforting arms.

# 4

## *Holiday*

Day was just dawning, the colourless sky waiting to be painted blue. Laura and Tim tiptoed around the house, managing with effort to suppress their excitement, talking in hushed whispers so as not to disturb Theresa, who was still sound asleep.

'Have you remembered to feed the fish? Mrs Simkins isn't coming in till tomorrow.'

'Have you watered your spider plants?'

'Mum, have you left a note for the milkman?'

'Did you cancel our comics?'

'I'm just going to say good-bye to the sunflower!'

'Can I play a last tune on the piano?'

'At six o'clock on a Sunday morning! No, of course you can't! No, not even a quiet one!'

At last all was ready, the car fully loaded, sleeping bags on the back seat, anoraks neatly folded on the back window, though it didn't look as if they'd need them.

Laura arranged a small pillow on Theresa's car seat, and Mum gently lifted the still-sleeping little girl into the car, wrapped in a woolly coloured-square blanket. She didn't stir. Laura had been worried at the thought of taking her on such a long journey, changing her surroundings yet again, when she was just beginning to settle down.

'Won't she wonder what's happening?' she had asked her mum late on Saturday night. 'She doesn't understand what a holiday is – she's never had one. Won't she be bored in the car? I hope she doesn't feel sick.'

'Yes,' agreed Mum, 'I'm concerned too, but I have prayed for her, and I feel sure God is looking after her. Would you like to pray for her too?'

'Yes, please,' said Laura sincerely. It had been a long time since she'd prayed with Mum. They used to do it every night when she was little. Then for several years she couldn't be bothered. Recently she had begun praying on her own again.

She and Mum had stood over the comfortable cot, with the bedroom door closed, and only the orange-coloured glow of the night light, and asked Jesus to help Theresa settle down quickly and be really happy with them. They had asked that she should be contented on the long journey to Wales, and not anxious and confused. They had asked that she should really enjoy the seaside and the sand and the animals in the country-side. Then Mum had opened her Bible and taken out an old well-worn postcard. On it was a picture of a sleeping new-born baby, wrapped in a white shawl, and beside it were the words:

'. . . these little ones . . . have their guardian angels in heaven, who look continually on the face of my heavenly Father.' Mathew chapter 18, verse 10.

Mum handed it to Laura. 'Would you like to keep it?' she asked gently. 'I've had it since you were a baby, and

I think it's written on my heart by now!'

Laura took the card and gave her mum a silent hug.
How good it was to know that God loved Theresa so
much that he sent his angels to watch over her.

By mid-morning Mum, Dad, Laura, Tim and Theresa
were well on the way to Wales. Theresa, snugly sand-
wiched between Tim and Laura, had slept for two hours.
She had woken up when they stopped for a picnic breakfast in a motorway service station carpark. She had
nibbled some sandwiches, had a drink of blackcurrant
juice and clutched her golden teddy, which Tim had
given her on the night of her arrival. Between the two
of them they managed to keep her occupied for the next
two hours of the journey too, with songs and tapes and
a bag of picture books and toy cars and little puzzles.

'What time is it, Dad?' asked Laura suddenly.

'Just on eleven,' he replied. Laura thought of all the
people back home at church. It seemed funny not to be
there on a Sunday. They would just be standing up to
sing the opening hymn, the organ playing loud rousing
chords. Laura loved the organ music and the singing
best of all. She and Mum went to church every Sunday,
Tim came most weeks, and Dad never came at all. Not
even when Laura was taking part in a Sunday School
Anniversary. And when they came back from a service
he was always rather snappy.

This was something Laura found very strange. If Mum
said it was all true, which she did, then why didn't Dad
believe it? And if Dad loved her so much, which she
knew he did because he always took her out and talked
to her and played with her and spent time with her, then
why wouldn't he come to hear her sing in church, not
even at Christmas?

She would have liked to make him answer her, and

she had tried asking several times, but all he said was, 'That's for you and your mum. I like my quiet Sunday mornings!'

When Laura was about seven, she had written her dad a letter one day, in painstaking printing and with a great deal of effort, because she never wrote much usually, telling him all about how Jesus had died on the cross for him and headed it:

'IT IS TRUE'

She had given it to her father on Easter morning, with an Easter garden she'd made in an old tin; with two wooden lollipop sticks for the cross, and with stones and moss and twigs and grass and little primroses and violets from the garden. It had been all her own idea. What became of the garden she couldn't remember. But he had thrown the letter in the bin. It had made Mum cry. Laura felt like crying too. Then the next day Dad had taken her out all day, as if to make up for it. Grown-ups were hard to understand.

'Come on, Laura,' said Tim, interrupting her wandering thoughts. 'Your turn to tell a story.'

Laura switched her attention back to Theresa and made up a story about a magic kitten who could talk and even sing! Theresa seemed to enjoy it, despite the fact that she had possibly never seen a kitten. They would be able to show her so many new and exciting things this holiday.

She wished the long journey were over. They were all beginning to get restless. Six hours was a very long time to spend in the car.

'See how many red cars you can see,' suggested Mum, but this became boring by the time they had reached a hundred.

'Look out for lorries from other countries,' said Dad,

as a juggernaut thundered past them, causing the car to shudder slightly for a moment or two.

'There's one from Portugal,' said Tim.

'I know a good game,' suggested Laura. 'For my breakfast this morning I had . . . then each person takes a turn and thinks of some food beginning with the next letter of the alphabet, in order. I'll start. For my breakfast this morning I had . . . an apple!'

'For my breakfast this morning,' continued Mum, 'I had an apple and a bacon sandwich.'

'For my breakfast this morning,' followed Tim, 'I had an apple, a bacon sandwich, a cream cake oozing with cream. . . mmmmmmmm. . . !'

'For my breakfast this morning,' added Dad, 'I had an apple, a bacon sandwich, a cream cake oozing with cream. . . mmmmmmmm. . . and a delicious doughnut!'

'Bekfast, 'smornin' had egg!' said Theresa seriously with Laura's help.

By the time the list had included fried fish, hamburgers, ice-creams, jelly and kippers, everyone was too confused to remember any more!

'Well,' said Dad, slowing to drive into the car-park of a roadside restaurant, 'I must say you've really put me off my lunch! Shall we just drive on?'

'No,' chorused Laura and Tim.

'No,' copied Theresa, with a little more force than usual, 'T'resa hung'y!'

Laura and Tim had hamburgers, chips and beans; and Theresa ate her chips with her fingers, dipping them first into a soft fried egg. For pudding there was a mix-up! Tim had ordered pancakes, but the waitress brought three ice-creams as well. In the end he finished off both and felt decidedly pleased with himself. He might be thin, but he had an enormous appetite!

When the family returned to the car, it was beginning to drizzle.

'I noticed the clouds building up as we travelled North,' said Mum.

'Oh, no,' moaned Laura, 'not rain on the first day of our holiday!'

'It *never* rains in Wales!' stated Dad with a grin. 'Repeat after me. . . .'

'It *never* rains in Wales,' chorused Tim and Laura.

''ever wains in Wales,' added Theresa.

'It's not rain,' continued Dad, determined to keep cheerful at any cost. 'It's sea-spray come in from the coast!'

'We're miles from the coast!' laughed Tim. 'Get your geography right, Dad. Long time since you were at school, isn't it?'

'Well, it's mountain mist,' said Dad, never stuck for an answer.

There weren't any real mountains in sight yet, but the children had noticed the change from flat countryside to rolling foothills with their sheep and streams and patches of purple rosebay willow herb. It was exciting, in spite of the rain!

'How many more hours?' asked Laura. 'I can't wait to get there!'

'Only about one,' said Mum with a smile.

'Aberdovey, here we come . . .' sang Dad, 'doodah, doodah . . .' and the children joined in, Theresa contributing her own version.

The roads became narrower and more winding and hilly. There were stone walls, with ivy and moss and little curling ferns, almost near enough to lean out and touch. At one point they were stuck behind a lorry and traffic was building up behind them, because it was impossible to overtake.

'Oh, I do like to be behind a lorry!' sang Dad, nothing able to quench his enthusiasm.

'What's holding us up now?' he asked later, as they crawled towards the sea. 'Is it a tractor, or a hay-lorry? Or,' he turned to grin at Theresa, 'is it a tortoise, or a giant snail?'

As they neared the coast, the clouds were left behind and the sun shone welcomingly. At last the sparkling waters of the Dovey Estuary came into sight through gnarled stunted little oak trees on the edge of the road, and here and there rowan trees added colour, with their berries just turning orange. On the other side of the road was a solid rock face, with some heather clinging in places and the odd yellow gorse bush finding just enough soil to grow in a crack. Further down the road were masses of blue hydrangeas, some in gardens and some seemingly wild.

The tide was in and dozens of brightly-coloured boats were bobbing about in the estuary. A breeze was rippling the waters, causing little white-tipped waves, and a gentle clanging, made by the wind in the masts and rigging, sounded almost like bells. Some yachts were decked out with red and yellow bunting and the harbour and the jetty were decorated with flags, as were the narrow winding streets.

Dad turned right, through the square, past the coffee shop, and then right again up a very steep and narrow hill. Up, up, up they went, the children gasping, the car engine working overtime, past little stone cottages with tiny gardens, and rows of terraced houses with doorsteps right onto the street. With a final heave, the car mounted the last and steepest slope and there they were, at the very end of the track, the highest point accessible by road, looking down on the hillside holiday village where they were to stay.

'Wow!' exclaimed Tim, gazing over the rooftops to the huge expanse of shining sea and sky. 'It's even better than I remembered!'

'Look, Theresa,' said Laura, cuddling the tired little girl in her arms, 'Seaside!'

Theresa pointed her finger. 'Seaside!' she repeated.

'And over there,' continued Laura, looking in the direction of miles and miles of sandy coastline, 'is the *beach*!'

Soon two brown heads were in sight, bobbing up the hillside steps, between bushes and waving grass, and Mark and Alice ran to meet their cousins.

'It's great,' shouted ten year old Mark. 'We've got that house,' pointing down to a large grey slate roof. 'It's better than last year! There's a patio and a balcony and a shower that works!'

Alice, who was eight, bounced up to Laura, her favourite cousin. 'You're sharing with me,' she shouted excitedly. 'Come and see our room. We've got bunk-beds and a huge cupboard, and our very own private door onto the patio! And there's a picnic bench and a sun-umbrella, and steps to a secret den. Come on!'

Laura, rather torn between exploring with Alice or looking after Theresa, finally kissed the sleepy child and handed her to her mother, who would best know how to look after her. Tim had already disappeared up the wild hillside with Mark. Apparently there was a cave somewhere hidden in the undergrowth.

Dad was having a good stretch after the journey, and Uncle Barry and Auntie Pam were helping with the luggage.

'This way,' said Barry, pointing down the steps. At the

end of the grey gravel pathway by a huge bush of blue hydrangeas, with heads as big as footballs, was the open door to their home for the next fortnight. This holiday was going to be fun!

# 5

## *Mark and Alice*

It was peaceful waking at the seaside – no traffic hum, no jet plane roar, no neighbours hurrying off to work. Laura lay still for a few moments in this strange silence, broken only by the cries of the seagulls.

Suddenly another song burst forth from the adjoining room:

'Heigh-ho, heigh-ho,
I think I've stubbed my toe!'

This was soon followed by the sound of splashing water, several 'ows' and 'ouches' and 'brrrs' – Barry was taking his early morning cold shower!

Laura smiled happily to herself, crawled to the end of her top bunk and just managed to stretch out and pull open the curtains. It was a calm and beautiful morning, blue sky, blue sea, golden sand, and, on the far side of the estuary, a patchwork of green and yellow fields, backed by the clear outline of the surrounding hills.

Alice emerged from a crumpled heap of bedding, and pulled herself up onto the top bunk to join Laura. She yawned dozily, pushed her brown hair out of her eyes, rubbed her freckly nose, and blinked in the sunshine.

'You can't take him anywhere!' she sighed, nodding in the direction of her father's shower. 'He never stops singing. At my party he told all the girls he was a retired pop-star!'

'Oh what a beautiful morning,
Oh what a beautiful day.
Good morning Laura and Alice –
How about coming my way?'

Six foot six inches tall, muscles like He-man, damp black curly hair, a moustache and large dark-rimmed spectacles – that was Barry looking round the door and inviting the two girls for an early morning stroll before breakfast.

Speedily they threw on jeans and sweat-shirts, tied their trainers, and left pyjamas and nightie strewn over the bedroom floor. A glimpse into Mum and Dad's room reassured Laura that Theresa was still fast asleep, despite the dawn concert, and Tim and Mark were obviously having a long lie after their late table-tennis match the evening before.

Laura and Alice hastily helped themselves to a drink of milk, leaving drips all over the kitchen worktop, grabbed a biscuit and rushed to join Barry on the patio where he was completing his keep-fit routine with deep-breathing exercises in the fresh sea air.

Because the village was built on a hillside, there were slopes or flights of steps everywhere. There were also banks and walls of tightly-packed grey slate, mined locally. Blending in with this were masses of rock plants and purple clover. In fact you stepped out of the front door to a haze of purple and blue, as spiky, strongly-scented buddleias stretched their arms out in all directions, tickling your face or brushing your hair as you strove to keep your balance on the steep and slippery paths.

The road down towards the harbour was just as steep, and Laura and Alice, as they skipped down hand in hand, felt their legs sort of aching and seeming most peculiar. They were both used to flat pavements everywhere at home. The view out to sea was now glimpsed through stone walls and over chimney pots, some of which were giving out wisps of smoke, despite the warm summer morning. As they neared the harbour, the smell of the sea and a salty, fishy tang grew stronger. Early morning fishermen had already been out in their boats.

'Wonder what they catch?' said Barry seriously. 'Of course, the waters round here *are* shark-infested, Laura, you do realise that?

Heigh-ho, heigh-ho, it's off to sea we go,

We'll throw young Laura to the sharks,

Heigh-ho, heigh-ho, heigh-ho!' he sang, as they reached the harbour railings and peered down into the depths of the clear dark green water.

Laura giggled and Alice shrugged her shoulders despairingly as her father sauntered off to the newsagents to buy a newspaper.

A group of boys had gathered at the foot of the jetty steps, on a small wooden landing-stage. They were peering at something in the water and uttering sounds of surprise and excitement.

'Come on,' said Laura, already beginning to climb down, 'let's see what they're looking at!'

Believe it or not, there in the sea was what looked like a real, no-kidding baby shark! It was dead, floating on the top, but nevertheless sinister enough to cause the girls to shudder. Ugh!

'I'm not swimming this holiday!' gasped Alice. 'Nor will Auntie Sue. She's even afraid of jelly fish!'

Laura was horrified. The very idea of having all this lovely sea, and not being able to swim and surf and dive. It was unbearable!

One of the older boys must have noticed her worried face, for he kindly explained that there were no sharks anywhere near the beaches or anywhere else for that matter! This was not a baby shark but a large dogfish which had been caught by a fisherman far out at sea. He had brought it back to the harbour, before dumping it overboard.

Laura and Alice breathed a sigh of relief.

'Let's trick your dad,' said Laura suddenly. 'Ask him what he'll give us if we find one of those sharks he was warning me about!'

Barry thought it was quite safe to promise the girls one pound each if they were able to find him a real shark. He soon became two pounds the poorer, fooled by the fin on the dogfish's back!

Giggling and laughing, and arm in arm, the girls ran back to the shop to spend their gains. Laura bought a red and yellow bucket and spade for Theresa, and Alice bought a crab-fishing line and hook. She liked fishing.

'Did I ever tell you the story of the crab?' asked Barry.

'No, no, no!' warned Alice forcefully. 'Don't let him tell you that one! It's horrible! You'll be awake all night!'

'We'll save it for bed-time,' said Barry with a gleam in his eyes.

Although there was always deep water in the harbour, the tide was actually about halfway out this morning, and the huge sweep of clean sand across much of the estuary looked very inviting.

'Let's go back across the sands,' said Barry. 'Then

we'll climb the steps at the other end of the village.'

Laura and Alice took off their trainers and fixed them to their belts. The sand was soft at first, squidgy and gritty between their toes. Soon, however, it became hard and firm, then ridged, deeper and deeper, in fact so deep it hurt their feet as they explored nearer to the bed of the river. Here and there were massive sandbanks, higher than the ridged parts. It was fun to run and leap and chase along them, then jump down the other side. Laura loved the freedom, the wind in her hair, the miles and miles of space around her.

'This is the life!' she called and turned several expert cartwheels. Alice followed her with handstands, and Barry suggested a game of leapfrog.

Suddenly Alice noticed that the ridges near to where they were playing were beginning to fill up with water. In a few moments they could actually see the tide running up the deep grooves in the sand, filling the channels and changing the larger sand-banks into much smaller ones.

'Quick,' said Barry, grabbing the girls by the hand, and pulling them across the sand so fast their feet hardly touched the ground. Every so often there was a stream to leap or ford, and the village still seemed very far away. Laura was frightened. It was incredible to see the sea rushing in so fast.

'It's all right,' reassured Barry. 'We're not in any danger, but we may get a bit wet!'

On and on they sped, dragged by Barry, who for once had no time for joking. Their arms hurt and they were panting for breath, and the channels they had to cross were becoming deeper and deeper. It was also confusing, because the sea seemed to sweep in from all angles and in odd directions. Laura pictured her mum and dad and Tim safely on land with little Theresa and wished she

41

were with them. The sea might be beautiful, but it was also powerful and treacherous.

At last the three found themselves with only one more channel between them and safety. It was, however, the deepest one of all, and Barry had to lift each girl in turn high on his strong shoulders, while he himself waded waist deep.

As they sat recovering on a seat by the river bank, watching the last sandbank disappear from view, Laura remembered to thank God for helping them back to safety.

'Well,' said Barry, 'that was adventure number one. I wonder what number two will be?'

'Here they are at last,' said Mum. 'The wanderers returned!'

'We almost drowned!' announced Laura dramatically. She looked at the smooth glassy sheet of water now completely covering the estuary, not a sandbank in sight. 'We were *under* there a few minutes ago!'

Both mums looked accusingly at Barry, who realised he had some explaining to do. Luckily Alice changed the subject.

'Where's our breakfast? I'm starving!'

'Sorry, none left,' replied Tim. 'Theresa has just fed the last crust to the birds. Save it from the seagulls if you can!'

Theresa was seated on the carpet by the open patio doors, watching, fascinated, as an enormous plump seagull waddled along the balcony railing and stopped to swallow a large lump of bread.

'Sammy Seagull! Sammy Seagull!' chanted Theresa, 'More b'ead, more b'ead!'

Mark ran to the kitchen, took several slices of fresh

bread from the bread-bin, broke them up and placed them in her eager chubby hands. Laura and Alice were interested too. They had never seen a seagull so close up and tame, with its fine white chest, wary eyes and sharp yellow beak. This time the impressive bird actually hopped from the railing to the balcony table. Suddenly, however, a flock of jealous jackdaws descended from a nearby fir tree. Ten or more there were, black and ugly, grey-headed and greedy, flashing their strange pale blue eyes, sharp beaks ready to steal and squabble and fight. Completely fearless, they swooped down right over the balcony. Sammy Seagull immediately took flight, and the jackdaws pinched the remains of the bread.

'Naughty jackdaws,' said Mark, putting his arm round Theresa.

'Shoo, shoo, you horrible birds!' shouted Laura, flapping her arms madly and managing to scare them away.

'I know,' said Alice, 'let's start a jackdaw watch. One of us has to be on duty to keep them away, so that Sammy and the other birds can have their food.'

'Huh, you've got a hope!' smiled Tim knowingly.

Mark persuaded his mother to let him have even more bread – all for the sake of keeping Theresa happy. The seagull didn't come back, but a blackbird pecked at crumbs only inches from the door, and two chaffinches with their pretty pink colouring fed happily a few feet away.

'Isn't it lovely here?' said Alice, as she and Laura finished off the bacon and eggs Mum had kept warm in the oven. 'All these tame birds, and this beautiful view! I wish I could live here for always!'

Theresa liked the new bucket and spade Laura gave her, and banged them together for a while like a drum. Without sand, however, buckets become boring, and

Laura was disappointed when the little girl soon discarded them. She found Mark's antics much more amusing, as he careered around the floor like a rollicking puppy, barking in her ears, hiding behind the sofa, popping out from the other end to surprise her and make her chuckle more than ever.

Tall and big, with the same dark curly hair as his father, Mark had inherited his sense of humour, although, unlike Barry, he had also a very serious side to his nature.

'Trust him to show off,' Laura muttered under her breath, as she went off to change into something cooler. Really she knew he was being kind, but Theresa belonged to *her*.

Alice followed Laura downstairs (it was a strange upside-down house, with a lounge on top and bedrooms beneath) and asked her cousin if she would like to see the 'den'. Laura pulled on her bright yellow shorts and top (her canary outfit as Tim called it) together with lemon coloured flipflops and was ready to go. Mum let them take Theresa with them, as long as they held her hand all the time.

Out they went, through their bedroom door which led onto the patio with the picnic table and sunshade, then down a steep and narrow flight of steps, round the corner, through a gap in an ivy-covered stone wall, and into an overgrown shrubbery. Alice held back the waist-high ferns, Laura carried Theresa, protecting her from any prickly branches. On and on they went through the undergrowth, a mixture of wild and garden plants, gorse, broom and heather until they reached a clearing, in the shape of a circle, so well hidden that no-one could possibly find them.

'Does Mark know about it?' asked Laura.

'No,' said Alice, 'I offered to show him where it was,

but he wasn't interested. He said he had a better place, a cave up somewhere on the hillside.'

'Good,' said Laura firmly. 'Then this is *our* secret — just you and me and Theresa.'

Laura stayed with Theresa while Alice went back to ask for some old car rugs and things to make the place cosy, because the ground was hard and the grass thin. Pam gave her a picnic basket too, as she said they weren't going out anywhere that day.

So the three of them munched and nibbled and chatted and relaxed in perfect secrecy, and called their den 'the robin's nest' (because a robin came and perched on a twig for a few moments). They decided to keep a notebook of all the beautiful nature things they found on this holiday.

Laura and Alice could have stayed there all afternoon, but Theresa became restless once lunch was over.

'Let's take her to the swings,' suggested Alice.

The children's play area was just beyond the houses.

Theresa's shrieks of joy made Laura warm inside too. She swung with her on her lap, she helped her struggle up the steps of the little slide and Alice caught her at the bottom, and together they bumped her up and down on the see-saw, her bright red dress puffing out in the breeze, showing her frilly white pants.

'Horsy, horsy, don't you stop . . .' sang Laura, as Theresa galloped backwards and forwards on the wooden rocking horse, and then held out her arms to be lifted down and try something else. Laura loved the warm soft arms around her neck. So much for Mark, she thought to herself with satisfaction. Theresa loves *me* best of all!

# 6

## *The forest trail*

'Today,' announced Mark importantly, waving a pile of maps, 'we're going on a "Barry and Mark Special", an expedition into the wilderness!'

'You've been warned, folks!' said Tim with a flourish of his long arms. 'Who knows! We may never return!'

'Oh,' moaned Laura, with a deep sigh, 'I want to go to the beach. Theresa hasn't seen the sand yet. *Why* can't we go to the beach? Why do we always have to do what *you* want to do? Anyway, Theresa's too young to go on one of your expeditions!'

'Dad's bought a kiddy-carrier for Theresa,' interrupted Mum, anxious that this should not turn into a family quarrel.

'I want to go to the beach too,' said Alice, who always supported her cousin. 'Let Mark and Tim go on one of their silly hikes.'

'No,' said Mum firmly, 'we're all going together, for the whole day, and taking a picnic. Who's going to help with the sandwiches?'

'Not me,' said Laura. 'I set the breakfast table.'

'And I helped,' added Alice. 'Why can't Mark or Tim do it?' But Tim had suddenly disappeared and Mark was too busy poring over maps with his father, and showing off his new expensive compass, and packing his storm-proof rucksack.

'You'd think we were going up Everest,' remarked Laura dryly, as she noticed his new leather walking boots, special thick knitted woollen socks, and, most comical of all, a red and white bobble hat!

'*You* might be glad of some boots before the end of the holiday,' said Dad, 'by the time we've walked you off your feet!'

'No fear!' said Laura. 'They make your feet look ten sizes bigger. Wellies are bad enough!'

'Anyway,' insisted Dad, 'it's cagoules today, and jeans or a track suit please, not shorts. Look at the mist outside. It's not going to lift before lunchtime.'

Sure enough, the view from the balcony this morning was completely hidden. Laura could see no further than the jackdaws' tree and the roofs of the houses directly in front. It was impossible to tell where the sea started or the sky finished. And the now familiar hourly chimes of the village clock sounded very dull and far away.

The next point of discussion was who should travel in which car. Laura liked driving with Barry and Pam, because they always joked and had fun and it helped to pass the journey. But if she went with Alice, then Mark would go with Tim – and that meant he would have Theresa. In the end Mark did go with Tim and Theresa, because he offered to map-read for his Uncle Rob. Cleverclogs again! As if *her* dad needed someone to map-read for him!

It was a shame about the mist. By all accounts the

journey *should* have been magnificent. Up, up, up they climbed on winding roads, through a narrow pass.

'The mountains here are over two thousand feet high,' said Pam, but all Laura and Alice could see was the fence at the edge of the road, a few rocks, the foot of a waterfall and several mournful, huddling sheep. It was hard to believe the peaks actually existed, when all you could see was clouds and swirling white mist. And everything seemed so damp. If you left the car window open, your hair started to feel wet.

'No wonder,' said Barry, at the highest point of the pass, 'we're actually *in* the cloud now.'

'Shall we ever find our way down?' he questioned dramatically, 'Or shall we be lost forever? Headlines – "The Misty Mystery of the Missing Travellers"!'

About an hour later, the two families reached a densely wooded area of hillside, parked the cars and set off on a forest trail. According to the map, the hike would be about five miles long and, at the furthest point, there were two hidden and spectacular waterfalls, reached only by footpath.

The mist still covered the mountains and hung in wisps around the treetops, and there was not another soul in sight. It was eerie and silent and mysterious.

Laura tied her cagoule hood tightly under her chin to protect her hair, and Alice did likewise. Theresa seemed cosy enough with a warm quilted suit, mittens and a furry bonnet, as she fitted snugly in the carrier on Dad's back.

First they strode along a narrow road, then turned left up a steep path through pine trees smelling sharply of resin. The trail was marked by painted red or yellow footprints, on posts by the wayside, and Theresa liked looking out for them, so the others let her spot them first. The trees were tall and straight, and rather brown and bare near the bottom, because of the lack of light. Underfoot were lots of broken twigs, dead leaves, brown pine needles, plenty of wet and slippery rocks and odd patches of very slippery mud. The track was extremely steep in places, and Laura looked for a walking stick among fallen branches in the undergrowth. Soon all four children had one and they proved very helpful for keeping their balance.

After a while they came out of the forest and took a path which followed alongside the edge of the trees steeply up and up till they reached a wider gravelly track, with recent tyre marks. It was obviously used by Forestry Commission workers. On the other side of this roadway was a steeply sloping field. The fog still hung low over the grass and plants and in places you could just make out that there was a further hillside beyond. In fact they seemed to be right in the middle of the mountains.

And still the track led up and up, through what seemed a weird wilderness of broken old trees, bare branches, half-trunks, stumps and spiky dead wood, waiting to be cleared for new little trees.

'Shh,' murmured Barry, with his finger on his lips. 'This is the territory of the wicked wizard of the woods! Don't disturb him anyone!'

'Help!' called out Alice, beginning to run. 'He's seen us! He's coming after us!'

Not exactly a beautiful place, thought Laura, but perhaps it would have been better in the sunshine.

And still they trudged on, on, on, without ever seeming any nearer to the top, or the end, or whatever else they were aiming at! Laura and Alice were becoming tired, and more than a little weary, and it didn't help when Dad told them they were nearly half-way to the falls now!

'Only half-way *there*!' exclaimed Laura. 'What about coming back?'

A change of direction, more footprints, white this time, and a white post with a number, led right into the darkest forest once more and a track you could hardly see, going steeply down-hill.

Mum and Pam looked very doubtful, but then reasoned that, in order to reach the waterfalls, they must keep on going down, and was that the sound of a river in the distance?

On this path it was very hard to keep your balance. It was slippery and rocky, slimy with wet dead leaves; there were fallen trees in the way, and vast squelchy patches of mud; and in some places the trail disappeared completely. Dad found it hard to cope with Theresa and the mums were slipping and sliding all over the place. Was it really the right way? The men and boys went on ahead to look.

When the party split in two, Laura began to feel really frightened and cross. Stupid fools! She knew they should have gone to the beach! Here they were in the middle of nowhere, in the thickest part of the forest. Lost. Trapped. What if a fire should start? Not likely with all this dampness, but what if they needed to get out in a hurry? Which way should they turn? It was impossible. What if someone was injured? What if there were adders? What if there were wild animals?

'God, where are you?' she screamed angrily inside her head. Panic, panic, panic. She knew he was there, but she couldn't *feel* him to be with her at all. It was just like those mountain tops covered with cloud. She believed they were there, but she couldn't see them. And she wanted to see them. She wanted proof.

At last there was a call and a whistling sound from deep down below them. It was Dad and Barry beckoning them on. A few minutes more and they saw them again, and heard clearly the sound of rushing water. Another fifty yards or so of zig-zag track and there they were at the bottom, on good solid ground once more, and the men were laughing hysterically over some sign or other. There was an arrow, pointing up the way they had just come, and a notice stating: Road closed – impassable.

From that point on everyone's spirits rose. Now the danger was over, the families could relax and enjoy a good laugh over their misfortunes. It would make an exciting story after all and, as Barry said, would certainly do for adventure number two!

'You kids were great!' he commented, patting them all on the back. 'You're really tough, all of you! Including Theresa. What a good little girl you've been!'

He handed out slabs of fudge, and Theresa finished hers swiftly and looked for more. Mark gave her his remaining piece, which Laura thought was rather generous. Perhaps her cousin wasn't so bad after all!

About a hundred yards further on, the track crossed an old curved stone bridge, and there, towering above them, was the first of the falls. The mist had by then lifted completely and the children stared up at this amazing sight. The river plunged over one hundred feet in a series of three fantastic drops. The top was so high, it hurt their necks to look up that far. And the light on the thundering white spray almost hurt their eyes, it was so bright. They had to shout to make themselves heard above the roar of the water, and the spray felt like a fine shower of rain.

Laura and Alice gazed at the thundering, pounding water, as if mesmerised. It was well worth all the effort of getting there. Theresa was fascinated. 'Bath,' she kept saying, never having experienced any other form of water.

'Somebody's tipped in a whole bottle of bubble bath!' shouted Tim, looking down from the bridge to the froth and foam below. On the other side the river flowed through a deep cut in solid rock. There it was smooth and clear and a deep amber colour, as was the large pool beyond.

Just round the corner was the second of the hidden falls, a wider one this time, though less deep, with a wall of cascading water. Then the two rivers merged in a series of bubbling turbulent rapids.

At a safer point the children all clambered down onto the rocks and threw stones into the water. Theresa sat down on Dad's anorak and played for ages with the smooth coloured pebbles, blues, mauves and greens. Everything was new and exciting for her, and her pleasure added greatly to that of everybody else.

'What a little darling!' remarked Barry.

'Isn't she good!' agreed Pam. 'Most two year olds would be a lot more trouble.'

'She's not used to getting much, so she doesn't ask for much,' replied Mum with a trace of sadness in her voice. 'It's all new to her though. She's coping very well.'

Laura looked on fondly. In the space of a few days she had grown devoted to the undemanding little girl. When the time came for her to go back, however would she do without her?

By then the sun was beginning to break through, and it certainly was a most beautiful place, completely natural and unspoilt.

'Why didn't we bring the picnic?' asked Alice suddenly. 'I'm starving.'

'So am I,' added Tim.

'Because,' replied Barry, 'for one thing we would have had to carry it all this way, and for another, we had no idea we would take so long.'

Mum had packed a drink for Theresa. It was in Mark's rucksack, together with some apples and bananas. But that was all they had.

'I suppose we'd better be going,' suggested Dad. 'Believe it or not, it took us two hours to get here, so we've a long walk back.'

'We can't go back the way we came,' said Mum with some determination.

'No,' said Barry. 'It's a circular route, and let's hope the next half is better!'

The first part was indeed much better. A steep, but firm and dry grassy pathway with rocks like steps up the side of another dark forest. The sun came glancing through the trees and it was all most pleasant. Later, however, when they again reached a wider way, it was a different story. All they could see ahead of them was a wide brown track of thick soft gooey mud – six inches deep and more in places, so that it almost came up to the top of their wellingtons. Trekking through it was like walking through glue.

'Told you we might be lost forever,' joked Tim. 'Can't you see it on the news? "Tired travellers trapped in treacle!" '

The grown-ups eyed each other in dismay. They were more than a little annoyed that the leaflet guide recommending this walk had not mentioned such hazards.

The thing which caused the most concern was that little Theresa was by then really tired and beginning to cry. No-one could bear to see her upset, but all they could do was to plod on.

Once again Laura felt an anger rise inside her. 'Did it *have* to end like this, God?' she demanded. 'Why did *you* let us come on this awful, horrible walk? Don't you care about little Theresa? If you *do* care, get us out of it!'

It wasn't a very respectful prayer, but it was honest, and it was soon answered.

Although they hadn't seen a single living person the entire morning, just at that moment came the sound of an engine slowly moving up behind them. It was a land-rover, easing its way, with difficulty, through the miles of mud.

Dad waved to the driver to stop, while the others moved out of the way to avoid splashes. He turned out to be the owner of the whole estate and he gladly offered Dad and Theresa a lift. Alice went too, and Laura was sorely tempted to join her. But Mark and Tim were continuing to the end, so she had to as well. She wasn't going to risk being called soft, not after all this effort.

Barry strode on ahead with Mark and Tim, while Mum and Pam and Laura got further and further behind. Mum put a comforting arm round Laura. 'You know, that was answered prayer for Theresa,' she said gently.

'Oh,' said Laura, 'did you pray too?'

'Yes,' said Mum, 'of course I did! And,' she continued, 'God has promised that those who trust in the Lord for help will find their strength renewed. I think we'd better pray for strength now.'

They did pray, but, quite honestly, Laura's feet felt just as heavy, and her legs just as aching and weary. She really didn't know how she could carry on.

'Let's try singing,' suggested Mum.

'Singing!' gasped Laura. 'I haven't got enough breath left to talk, never mind sing!'

'It's worth a try,' said Mum. 'Perhaps if we sing to God in thanks for his strength, we shall feel it flowing into us.'

Laura reckoned it was a dumb idea, but by this time she was desperate. So when Mum and Pam started singing a chorus, she sang too:

'When the road is rough and steep,
Fix your eyes upon Jesus.
He alone has power to keep.
Fix your eyes upon him.
Jesus is our greatest friend,
One on whom we can depend.
He is faithful to the end.
Fix your eyes upon him.'

It was incredible, but it worked. The way seemed just as long, but Laura had new bounce in her step and strength in her body, and, as their voices rang through the lonely woodland, she felt peace and hope in her heart once more.

Dad held out his arms to welcome them back to the cars, and Laura flopped into them, exhausted but triumphant. She had finished the course, and it was certainly a lot longer than the five miles mentioned in the leaflet!

The children paddled in a nearby river to clean their boots – Alice cleaned the inside as well as the outside by going too deep – while the mums set out lunch on a wooden picnic bench under the pine trees. Already little birds – chaffinches and blue tits – were gathering in the hope of crumbs.

The journey back was glorious. Laura drove with Mum and Dad and Theresa and Alice this time.

'Look at these mountains,' she enthused. 'Dad, stop the car and look at those mountains! They're gigantic.'

Dad pulled into a lay-by and they all gazed up at the

magnificent peaks clearly outlined against the now bright blue sky.

'They're massive,' said Laura. 'I can't get over them!'

'We're not asking you to,' said Dad. 'We'll save that for another day!'

# 7

## *Shell Island*

'Yippee!' cried Laura, grinning from ear to ear, 'I beat him, I actually beat him!'

Mark was left standing at the table-tennis table wondering what had hit him, and Laura was leaping jubilantly along a lowish stone wall to tell her mother.

'Well done,' said Mum, as she pegged Theresa's washing on the line, 'but don't let it go to your head!'

Laura bounced up some steps, turned the corner without looking and bumped straight into a lady who reminded her of Great Aunt Maude.

'Manners, my girl!' exclaimed the elderly holiday-maker, adjusting her pink spotted dress.

'Sorry!' called back Laura, without even stopping. 'Batty old bird!' she muttered under her breath.

Anxious to add victory to victory, Laura gladly agreed to a game of cricket on the sands by the harbour, while the mums prepared for the day's outing.

It was Dad, Tim and Laura against Barry, Mark and Alice, and both sides were in deadly earnest. Mark batted first and gained a respectable forty-one runs, Alice scored twelve and Barry fifty-seven.

Laura took hold of Mark's heavy full-size bat and positioned herself in front of the wicket. She glanced up to the cloudless blue sky, as if that would help! Success breeds success, so they say, and certainly Laura was on top form after her early morning win. Her first ball was a six and she didn't need to run. She then scored several more sixes and some fours, followed by a fantastic shot that reached the lapping tide-line waves. A few more feet and it would have been lost for good!

'Look at sloggerchops!' called Barry. And she needed only two more runs to beat Mark's score!

Then it happened – a very awkward ball from Barry, a whacking good hit from Laura – too high though, disastrously high – ending in a perfect catch by Mark! Out! He had beaten her by one run.

Laura's family still won the match, because Tim excelled himself and Dad did better than usual. But Laura wasn't interested. She shuffled her feet around in the sand waiting for the game to end, and sulked all the way back to the house. Even Alice didn't want her company, realising that her cousin was in one of her moods!

And so it would have continued, were it not for a lucky distraction.

'Help!' called Mum from her bedroom window as they neared the house. 'There's a bird in here, and I don't know how we're ever going to catch him.'

Theresa was shrieking delightedly, 'Birdie, birdie, birdie in house!' Pam was standing beside her in the doorway white-faced saying, 'Don't panic, Sue!' and Mum was squashed up against the bedroom window terrified of the tiny flapping object winging its way madly from wall to wall.

Mark and Laura reached the room first, and Mark immediately took charge.

'Close the curtains,' he said, 'so he won't batter himself against the glass trying to get out. Now just go away everybody and leave him to calm down.'

Everyone left except Laura, who sat down quietly by the door waiting to see what would happen. The two of them were silent for some time and the frightened little bundle of feathers, with its heart beating twice as fast as normal, stopped flying around and disappeared under the bed.

After some time Laura lifted the cover and had a peep. The little creature had stopped panicking, and soon felt brave enough to hop out into the light.

'It's a robin,' whispered Mark.

'I think it's the one we fed the other day,' said Laura. 'I've seen it around all over the place. It's ever so tame.' She gazed at the bird with its bright eyes, sharp beak, lovely orangey red chest and long brittle legs. All fluffy and fat it was.

'Must have hopped in the open window from the bushes outside,' said Mark.

Without saying a word, both knew that the other cared deeply about the little bird and, for the time being, a silent bond was formed between them. The robin seemed to have lost its fear and hopped happily from place to place, over the green and white bedcover, pausing on the pillows, standing still a few seconds on Mum's green leather Bible!

Laura thought to pray for its safety and that it would find its way out into the sunshine again, and it was at that point she came up with a brilliant idea. She sent Mark off for some biscuit and bread crumbs and laid a trail from the bed to the wall, and along the sill to the open window. The robin tried one (watched now by Alice and Theresa as well) found it a bit hard, and disappeared under the bed again. Patiently the children waited for him to emerge, and the next time he followed the food exactly as planned, fluttered up on the sill, noticed the open window and hopped out.

'Whew!' said Mark. 'Thank goodness for that!'

'Thank you, God,' said Laura inside her head.

She couldn't help comparing Theresa with the robin – helpless and frightened at first, then trusting and sweet.

The children went upstairs to the balcony to feed the other birds. Sammy Seagull was waiting eagerly, Betty Blackbird was perched on the back of a chair and a pair of chaffinches were pecking round the door. It was lucky there were no jackdaws that morning, as the children had completely forgotten about the jackdaw watch.

Every scrap of bread was speedily devoured, and the girls noted it all down in their nature note-books, before the families set off on the day's outing.

'Today,' announced Dad, 'we're taking you to an island!'

'A real island?' questioned Laura. 'Do we go by boat?'

'Yes, a real island,' answered Dad, 'but no, no boat!'

'But how can we go to an island without a boat?' persisted Alice.

'We go across a causeway, that's a narrow strip of land,' explained Mum, 'at low tide. When the tide comes in, we'll be cut off from the mainland. Then we have to wait until low tide again to go back. That's why we're spending all day there.'

'Good,' smiled Laura. 'That sounds better than forest trails.' She turned to Theresa. 'We're going to the beach,' she said. 'You can play with your bucket and spade.'

'She'll like it,' said Mum. 'There are two beaches, a sandy one and a rocky one; and *you'll* like the rocky one – it has hundreds of different shells.'

'Hundreds?' queried Alice.

'Yes,' said Dad, 'apparently two hundred different varieties have been collected there. That's why it's called Shell Island.'

At last they turned off the main road, crossed a railway line at the level crossing, and continued down the narrow lane which led to the sea. The children soon spotted the causeway – a narrow raised track, rocks placed each side, across what seemed like a reedy, marshy stretch of sand. The tide was already covering some of the mudflats, but the road was quite clear.

Laura gazed out of the open window. It was a strange place – wild, but exciting, and very lonely with mountains towering behind and further mountain ranges just visible beyond the bay.

There was a breeze blowing too, sending white clouds scudding across the skyline. Breezes and mist and adventurous empty places all seemed to be part of Wales.

The cars were parked on a stretch of short springy grass with only the odd sheep for company. Though, judging by the holes in the sandy hillocks nearby, there were rabbits around too.

Laura zipped up Theresa's anorak, pulled a red sweatshirt over her own head, and they made their way, followed by the others, down onto the rocks by a steep stony path. Each had a polythene bag for collecting and Theresa was holding tightly to her new red and yellow bucket and spade. Mum laid a thick groundsheet on the shingle and sat down with the little girl, who immediately began shovelling away contentedly, while the others went exploring.

'Can't see many rare shells yet!' called out Laura, above the wind. 'Thought there were hundreds!'

'They won't jump up into your hands,' replied Tim, his hair blowing all over his forehead. 'You've got to hunt for them.'

Certainly the pools were full of blue and black mussels, white or beige, frilly-edged cockles, dark knobbly winkles and pointed hat limpets clinging so tightly you would need a knife to prize them off the rocks. There were also empty whelks, some very large, but mostly broken, and piles of long shiny, purple-patterned razor-shells, some single, some still joined as a pair. Mark found a really huge, bumpy, unbroken oyster. Trust him to be the first, Laura thought. Tim found a large, smooth, yellow shell which they'd never seen before. Then Alice found a scallop, pearly purple inside and perfectly ridged outside in patterns of pink and brown. She was very pleased with herself! Only Laura had found nothing unusual so far, and this wasn't exactly pleasing her.

'It's not fair,' she muttered, wandering off on her own and stepping from boulder to boulder grumpily. 'Why do they have all the luck?' She jumped down onto a damp patch of shingle and crunched the shells sullenly beneath her feet. Had she but stopped to look properly there might have been several varieties lurking there, but patience was not Laura's strong point.

Then she saw it! And gave a scream of terror which resounded across the rocky bay and made the others leap and bound over seaweed and rockpools to reach her.

It was the most gigantic crab Laura had ever seen! And it had sidled out from under a large rock right next to her, with its horny brown shell and evil-looking pincers and claws.

'It's B..B..Barry's crab!' she shrieked, remembering the story her uncle had told them only the night before, about this ancient, wicked crab who had bitten him and slowly, chillingly turned *him* into a crab! Alice had warned her not to listen to it!

'Don't be stupid,' scolded Tim. 'It was only a made-up story! You know it wasn't true!' But, all the same, he stopped still and shuddered in amazement at the giant speciment right beside Laura's foot. He held out his hand and heaved Laura up to safety on a high rock and the four of them stood peering down at the monster below them. Slowly Laura's fears subsided and she began to giggle with relief.

'Your dad's too good at telling stories,' she commented to Alice and Mark. 'One of these days I'm going to find something to give *him* a shock!'

Shell collecting seemed tame and pleasant after that, and Laura was delighted to be the first to find several small and perfectly shaped sunset-shells. They were smooth and delicate, yellowish white in colour, with purple rays, just like a beautiful evening sky. Thank goodness for pretty things, thought Laura. Or rather, thank God. She shared her shells with the others, and they, in turn, gave her a twirly-top shell with a mother of pearl lining and a tiny attractive bright pink shell, which Mark looked up in a pocket book, and said was a Baltic tellin.

Suddenly Tim noticed Barry waving energetically at them from the grass at the top of the beach.

'Must be lunchtime at last,' he said.

'Great!' said the others and were soon bounding towards the cars.

They spread themselves out on groundsheets and rugs and were soon munching away at ham and cheese and salad rolls, with crisps and peanuts. There were chocolate biscuits and apples and bananas to follow.

After lunch, Theresa proudly showed her bucket full of stones and shells, and the others looked through them with her. Suddenly Mark picked up a minute spiral shell. 'Gosh,' he said, 'look what she's found. It's a wentletrap!' The others looked suitably impressed, and told Theresa what a clever girl she was. More delving in the bottom of her bucket unearthed, or rather unsanded, a pyramid-shell, a tusk-shell, a beer-barrel and a cowry, all less than a centimetre in height!

'Where did you find them, Theresa?' asked Laura.

'Beach,' said Theresa with a beaming smile and pointing her finger. 'S'ells on beach!'

The others let Theresa show them where she had been sitting, and they settled themselves down beside her to scrabble about in the shingle. Once they really started searching, they uncovered dozens of minute specimens.

'I know,' said Barry, with his usual flourish, 'we'll have a grand competition for the best shell collection by the end of the holiday! Prizes too! The first one will be something really valuable!'

The children eyed the contents of their polythene bags, and wondered who had the most shells so far.

'And,' continued Barry, 'marks will be given for presentation and naming too, so that should keep you all busy! And extra marks for anything really original and rare!'

By mid-afternoon, the wind had dropped, the sky was clear blue and the sun was hot. Tim and Mark were keen to move further round the island where the rocks gave place to a stretch of smooth golden sand, and the surf crashed in because of the flatness.

All changed into swimsuits, including Theresa. Tim,

Mark, Laura and Alice pounded over the firm, wet sand and dashed straight into the breakers. With squeals and yells and splashing and dodging, they chased each other in and out of the white foam. Deeper and deeper they went, until the swell almost lifted them off their feet, and all you could see, when a big wave came, were four bobbing heads, which Laura's mum kept counting, not relaxing until Rob, Barry and Pam were changed ready to join them.

Mum took Theresa to paddle at the edge, but she was afraid of the waves, and drew back each time one lapped round her toes. Instead Mum began to dig her a little pool which quickly filled with water of its own accord and kept her perfectly safe and happy.

Alice soon joined her, having had enough of the boisterous sea, and Laura was next to come on shore, after one very large wave had crashed right over her head, making her eyes sting and giving her more than a taste of salt water. She rubbed her hair dry with a towel, changed into shorts and a T-shirt and began building a sand boat for Theresa.

It was a marvellous model, expertly shaped, firmly patted down, with two seats, a frisbee for a steering wheel and white cockle shells for controls. By the time Laura had finished the digging, she was quite exhausted and ready to flop down on a towel for a rest.

Then Mark came running up, fresh and invigorated from his swim, showing off about six-foot waves and how he stood up against them. Without even stopping to ask whose boat it was, he leapt into the front seat, made the most ridiculous speedboat sound effects and took Theresa for an imaginary trip round the bay!

The little girl chortled with delight, while Laura's face turned to thunder. How dare he? Didn't he realise all the effort she'd put into it? It was her idea, and now he would get all the credit for it.

'If you don't mind,' she fumed, '*I* built that boat and *I*'m going to drive it!'

Mark got out and Laura stepped in, but she wasn't in the mood to utter quite such loud engine noises and soon Theresa was calling out, 'Mark do it! Mark do it!'

That was the last straw. To have Theresa actually preferring Mark to her! Laura felt tears rising in her eyes, and went for a walk along the beach so that no-one else would notice. All she could think of was how Mark was purposely taking Theresa away from her, and she *hated* him.

Laura paced further and further away from the others, her anger growing with every step. He was too big, that boy, too big for his boots. Big and bossy and b . . . b . . . b . . . (Laura struggled for words) blow him! She picked up a piece of driftwood and wrote in largest of letters on the sand for all the world to see: 'I hate Mark!' and underlined it.

Just as well for her it was her own dad who came to fetch her, and not Barry. Miserably Laura joined the others once more, as they set off back across the causeway again, over the level crossing and onto the road home.

Before they climbed the hill up to the house, however, they stopped in the village to visit the shell shop. Here were row upon row of ornaments and jewellery made almost entirely from shells. Some were natural and others had been painted and varnished. Some were made into sailing boats, others into animals. There was even a model lady with a beautiful long shell skirt. There were pictures made from shells, there were dishes decorated with shells, there were baskets of beautiful large exotic foreign shells – Laura noticed Barry looking at those and wondered whether some of them would be the prizes for the competition. In one corner was a collection of shell boxes, made from polished wood, lined with satin, the lid and sides decorated lavishly with all sorts of exquisite tiny shells, some similar to those Theresa had found that day.

Laura noticed Theresa looking at them again and again, holding one with care, and help from Mum, and peeping inside. Clearly she thought they were wonderful. When the time came to leave, Mum had to force the little girl to open her clutching fingers and let go her grip on a small and extemely expensive one.

'That's not for you, darling,' she explained kindly. 'It's not suitable. Costs too much money – too easily broken!' And it was not without a lot of cajoling and several tears that they took her out of the shop.

Mark had been watching too and lingered to look again at that box – and the price tag! If only it had been cheaper!

He would have gladly bought it for her. Perhaps by the end of the holiday – if he saved all his money? And tomorrow was Saturday, pocket money day. He would think about it.

# 8

## The beach

'Come on, Laura,' pleaded Alice. 'Please, please come! We've booked a pony for you.'

'Oh, sure,' said Laura sarcastically, 'I suppose you all want a good laugh when I fall off and break my leg, do you? I told you, I'm useless at riding.'

'Thought you'd never been before,' persisted Alice, 'so how d'you know?'

'I'm *not* going to give Mark the chance to show me up any more! He's bound to be brilliant.'

'Actually,' replied Alice, 'he's not! Last time we went riding his pony threw him in the mud right at the end of the ride!'

Laura looked up, at last showing a spark of interest.

'Did he really?' she asked. A faint grin spread over her face. 'O.K. I'll come after all!'

The sight of Barry on a horse – cart-horse variety – was enough to make anybody laugh. Alice had the smallest pony, called Bracken, and Laura the second smallest – a shiny chestnut brown called Brandy. She loved animals, and was glad she had decided to come this fine sunny morning. The guide held her on a leading rein for a little way, as this was her first ride, but soon she was able and confident enough to go on her own. She had a good sense of balance and felt quite relaxed. So did Tim. Alice seemed very experienced and natural. Mark, on the other hand, was stiff and tense.

'Hope he falls off again,' said Laura to herself as they mounted a hillside. 'Would serve him right for being such a show-off!'

The group reached the top of the ridge and stopped to gaze at the view. It was good to feel the wind on your face, and breathe in the fresh early morning air, and you could see far out across the estuary, even further than from their hillside house. Just one huge expanse of blue, quiet and still and glistening in the sunshine.

Down the other side was a small reeded lake, and a strange valley where every sound echoed again and again. Laura gave Brandy a pat. It was great to see all those places without having to walk.

So far the horses and ponies had only walked. On the way back, however, the guide let some of them try trotting. Laura was thrilled to find that she could do it, and was soon well in front with Alice, bobbing up and down rhythmically in the saddle, while Tim was in the middle and Mark was left far behind. This would teach him a lesson. Perhaps he would leave Theresa alone today. But in case he didn't, Laura had worked out a plan. As soon as they got back, she and Alice would pack a bag of things to do and take Theresa off to their secret den. They would be spending a quiet day today, because Barry and Pam were preparing for a climbing expedition on Sunday.

Later, the children walked back down to the house,

had a drink of squash and some biscuits and then the girls and boys separated. Mark and Tim were obviously heading for their hillside cave, with a stock of sandwiches and crisps, while Laura and Alice decided they would bring Theresa back for lunch and enjoy it on the patio under the big blue and yellow sunshade.

By late afternoon, however, the groups met up again at the games room, where there was, in addition to table-tennis, a new full-size snooker table. Laura loved snooker. Recently she'd spent hours playing with her dad and had become really expert. She just couldn't wait to smash through that triangle of glowing red balls, on the bright green felt.

'I'll break,' she cried, picking up the shortest cue.

'You're on,' replied Mark, not imagining that his cousin would give him much of a challenge.

By the time Laura had snookered him three times, and after she had potted most of the red balls and was beginning on the remaining colours, he began to change his mind, and was more than a little annoyed. After all, she was only a girl! She'd beaten him hollow at table-tennis, and taken the lead in pony-trekking. If she beat him at snooker too, he'd never live it down! He couldn't afford to let her win another competition. Where on earth had she been practising?

Mark came up with two ideas to save face. Either he must jog the table, move all the balls, and stop the game. (But that would be pretty obvious and besides the table was heavy.) Or else he must pretend he was holding back to give her a chance, in fact kindly *letting* his cousin win.

Purposely he missed two easy shots. Then purposely and obviously he potted the white ball, thus losing four points, all the time larking around, making a complete fool of himself, giving the impression it wasn't really worth trying when playing with her. Laura was furious!

'Keep you hair on,' laughed Mark. 'You're not Steve Davis, you know! It's only a bit of fun!'

'Relax, can't you,' added Tim. 'We're supposed to be on holiday. What does it matter?'

It was the same at school. No matter what happened, other people always seemed to come off on top! If she lost – they would make fun of her for losing. If she won – fairly and squarely and with a great deal of effort – they were jealous and would shrug it off and ridicule her for taking it so seriously. One-upmanship! That's what it was called. And it was a skill Laura had not yet learned to master.

Laura stormed off up to the house, keeping her mouth shut only with difficulty. She felt just like a firework ready to explode, or a volcano about to erupt. Tim often called her Spitfire. No doubt the boys would have been really amused to see her in a proper rage.

Back at the house, Theresa had finished her tea and Mum was rubbing her dry in a large towel after her bath. Laura gave her a hug and rested her angry face against the warm cuddly sweet-scented little body. Chubby arms came out from under the towel and Theresa gave Laura a welcome hug.

'Story, story – p'ease story!' she said.

Laura dried between her toes, dusted her with talc, popped a pink nightie over her curly head and carried her off to bed. She could easily have made up a story about how unkind children were and how unfair life was, but she stuck to 'The Three Bears' instead. Then she tucked the covers cosily around the little girl and began a lullaby.

She was just about to tiptoe from the room, when a

plaintive little voice murmured, 'Sing Bimbi, oh, p'ease sing Bimbi.' Laura looked puzzled.

'Bimbi?' she asked. 'What's Bimbi?'

'You know,' persisted Theresa, becoming almost upset at the lack of understanding. 'Bimbi, Bimbi, *Bimbi!*'

Laura went through all the lullabies and bedtime songs she knew, plus several nursery rhymes, only to hear a disappointed, 'Dat not Bimbi!' each time.

Finally she tried:

'Jesus loves me, this I know,
For the Bible tells me so,
Little ones to him be . . .'

'Yeh, dat Bimbi!' came Theresa's cry of relief and delight, and she settled down to sleep.

Sleep was more than Laura could do that night. Although Theresa had calmed her down considerably, she was still angry inside and bitter about the unfairness of it all. The next thing would be the shell competition. Mark would be sure to have a superb collection – and win. And tomorrow Barry and Pam were going on their mountaineering trip from dawn till late at night, and her parents had offered to take all the children for a picnic on the beach. That meant being with Mark all day, with no chance of getting away from him at all.

Laura didn't feel like praying, but she did just murmur, 'God bless Theresa and keep her safe.' Whatever happened, she couldn't leave that out. At that moment Theresa was the most precious thing in the whole world to her.

The next day was bright and clear and promised to be a scorcher. Not a cloud there was in the wide, wide sky, just perfect blue from corner to corner.

Dad parked the car in a lay-by on the winding roadside

and the children tumbled out of the back, for it had been quite a squash.

'How do we get to the sea, Auntie Sue?' asked Alice, shielding her eyes. She could see it shining and shimmering, but in between seemed miles of sand-dunes.

'It's not that far,' reassured Mum. 'We go over the level crossing, then take that path across the golf-course,'

'Told you I should have put in my clubs,' said Mark to Alice.

'Oh, no,' moaned Laura, hand on head, 'not another of his many skills and achievements!'

'Everyone has to carry something,' called Dad, handing out bags and towels, and bats and balls and spades, 'and I'll carry Theresa!' He popped a white frilly sunhat on her head. It matched the trimming on her blue sundress. 'Beautiful!' he announced. 'The belle of the beach!'

Tim read out the notices by the railway line. Whistles warned of an approaching train, it said, and, just at that moment, a loud piercing note sounded from down the track.

'Stand well back, everyone,' called Mum, and Laura covered Theresa's ears with her hands in case she should be frightened. The monster roared past, causing everyone to shudder, and Theresa hid her face in Dad's shirt.

Next came the hazard of flying golf balls. 'Wait,' announced Dad, holding up his free arm. 'They're just about to tee off on the green.' Mark watched interestedly, Laura and Alice looked bored, and Tim was impatient, for he longed for his swim in the sea. Mum picked Theresa some pretty yellow and purple wayside flowers.

Finally came the obstacle of the sandhills. Close at hand they seemed more like mountains, and steep ones at that. From then on the landscape was painted in three colours only – blue sky, pale soft yellow sand, and tall tough green grasses.

'Best to take off your shoes,' called Dad, stopping to unfasten his. The sand got in everywhere. Bare feet sunk in deeply and they struggled on towards the top. It was pleasant, though, warm and fine and easily brushed off, and good to feel between your toes.

Theresa held on tightly to her bucket and spade and jiggled around excitedly in Dad's arms. She remembered the sand from Shell Island, and couldn't wait to get stuck into it again!

'Let's stop here,' called Laura and Alice, pointing to a sheltered valley between two dunes, and a path which eventually led over one more hillock to the open beach.

'Fine,' agreed Mum, and they all dropped their bags and bundles and spread out the groundsheets and blankets to make a base. The children changed into shorts or swimsuits and were eager to race down to the sea, until Dad pointed out how far away it was! They stood and gazed from the top of the last sand-dune over an expanse of miles of smooth, flat, empty sand in every direction. Deserted, apart from themselves and the gulls. Its vastness was quite overwhelming.

'The tide is out at its very lowest point now,' explained Dad. 'Wait until it's on the turn. Then it comes in very quickly. Leave it for an hour or so. We'll still have a long walk, but not as long as this!'

The children all joined in to dig a huge hole for Theresa to play in. Round the edge they hollowed out seats, and shelves, and then Laura had the idea of making it a baker's shop for her. With help, Theresa managed to make pies in a small bucket and tip them out on the smoothly patted sand. And Laura and Alice made cakes and decorated them with seagulls' feathers, then bought them with pebble and shell money they had collected, and pretended to eat them – and Theresa loved it.

The sun was growing hotter and hotter. The sand felt so burning you could almost fry an egg on it, thought Laura, a sandy egg! With breadcrumbs! Mum made sure the children covered themselves well with suntan lotion, for there was no shelter anywhere.

After a while Laura and Alice took Theresa to hunt for shells. Most they put into her bucket, but any special ones they kept for their own collections. Alice found one no-one had ever seen before. It was like a small whelk, though smoother and more dainty and attractive and with a spread-out fan-shaped opening. Mark looked it up in his shell guide and decided it was a pelican's-foot. The others were quite envious.

Then Laura had the idea of rolling a ball down a high sand dune, first making a track for it to follow by pushing aside the soft sand. Theresa loved catching the ball at the bottom and Alice tirelessly carried it to the top again. The girls then decided it might be fun to roll or slide down the slopes themselves.

'Whee!' screamed Alice, 'Watch out, everyone! I can't stop.' Mum lifted Theresa out of the way.

'Help!' shrieked Laura, as she leapt down in huge, uplifted bounds. She felt as though she might take off in flight at any moment.

'I know,' suggested Tim, 'let's have a longjump competition.'

The children smoothed the sand and marked out a starting line. Each person's jump was recorded by a cricket stump or a spade. Dad was the funniest of them all, taking a long run first and panting and snorting with effort, thundering down towards the jumping line like an escaped elephant.

Laura and Alice did quite well, though Mark did better. Mum never managed to take off at all, but Laura was pleased to note that her brother, with his long thin legs, jumped much the furthest of all.

'Can we go in the sea yet?' asked Laura.

'Yes,' said Dad, looking at the tide. 'It seems to have come in a hundred yards or so. We'll go now.'

'Coming to paddle in the sea?' Mum asked Theresa.

'No,' said Theresa firmly with a shake of her head. 'No sea!'

'All right,' agreed Mum. 'We won't bother with your swimsuit. Just come down and play at the edge.'

The soft sand soon gave place to firmer sand with a long ridge of shells and stones and seaweed and driftwood at high-tide mark. After that there was nothing but smooth firm wet sand, with the odd isolated shell or pebble. It seemed to stretch for ever. Behind them was a backdrop of mountains and on each side, in the far distance, were ranges of high peaks. Somewhere among them were Barry and Pam tackling a rock face, perhaps, on their way to the summit.

Laura and Alice danced and skipped and flung their arms around. It was so wonderful to have all this space, all to themselves. As they neared the sea, the sand became ridged and harder on their feet, and there were shallow pools of cool refreshing water.

The sea itself, when finally reached, was clear and calm, only little waves at the edge to jump over. It was icy cold, however, and there were shoals of tiny fish.

The children ran and leapt and splashed through the shallows, and Theresa lost her fear and wanted to join in. Mark came up and took her by the hand and jumped her over the ripples.

'More sea, more, more, more,' she called out happily, skipping and dancing and singing a little song to herself.

'Oh, dear!' said Mum, eyeing her splashed pants and the damp hem on her sundress, 'I should have taken her swimsuit! I haven't even got a towel for her.' She looked back the way they had come with a reluctant sigh. The sand-dunes were so small and low in the distance, they seemed miles away. 'I suppose I'd better go back and get them.'

She looked around for Dad, but he had already gone swimming with Tim and Laura, Laura being anxious to be the first one right in, to beat Mark. She hesitated for a moment, then looked at her nephew. 'Would you mind looking after her?' she asked. 'I'm afraid I won't be very quick.'

'No, that's all right,' said Mark helpfully. 'I'll take care of her till you get back.'

'So will I,' said Alice. 'I don't want to go deep anyway.'

Mark looked over at Uncle Rob and his cousins. They seemed to be going further and further out to find water deep enough for a good swim. Evidently they had just found it, judging by the kicking of legs and the three heads moving across the smooth surface. It was an ideal day for a swim, calm as a mill pond. Usually the waves got in the way. Mark looked back at Sue's receding figure. Goodness, she had a long way to go. He hoped she would hurry. At this rate the others would be coming out by the time he got in.

Laura and Tim were having a marvellous time, and never stopped to look back. Tim's strokes were so strong, you'd think he could reach Ireland!

'Isn't it fantastic?' shouted Laura, wiping the splashes from her face, still leaving drops on her long dark eyelashes. 'I'm so happy. Look how far I've swum! Dad, watch me! I can do backstroke in the sea! Watch me, Dad!' Laura lay back and let the salty water take her full weight. She licked her lips, and tasted its tang, and felt the warm sun on her face. She kicked her legs faster to move more quickly, her whole body fresh and cool and bursting with energy and enthusiasm.

'Dad, can we come again tomorrow? Dad, can you teach me how to dive? Dad, can we stay in for hours?'

Mark, meantime, held Theresa's hand tightly to stop her sitting down in the water, though she was so wet it wouldn't have made much difference. It was hard work looking after a toddler all on your own. Also Alice was complaining of getting cold and wanted to go back. Then Theresa grew tired of waiting for Mum and decided *she* wanted to go back. Mark didn't know what to do. Come what may, he was determined not to miss his swim.

'I'll take Theresa back,' offered Alice suddenly. 'We'll probably meet Auntie Sue on the way down and save her a journey.'

'All right,' agreed Mark. It sounded like sense. It would save his aunt all that walking for nothing, now that Theresa no longer needed her swimsuit. Mark looked once more to see if he could attract his uncle's attention, but all three were far too busy; and then he handed Theresa over to Alice and told her to keep in a straight line up the beach and she couldn't go wrong.

It was easy to say, but actually keeping a straight line in a vast expanse of country all looking exactly the same, was really far from easy, even for a grown-up. Mum had found it hard enough and ended up several sand-dunes to the right of where she was supposed to be. It was only when she stood on a very high dune, that she managed to spot her checked blanket still spread out in the sun. She was so exhausted that she had to sit down for a rest and a drink before setting off again with a towel and Theresa's swimsuit.

As she finally neared the sea once more, she strained her eyes to pick out Mark and Alice and Theresa, but could see no figures at all by the water's edge. At first she thought she must be off course again, but she still could see no-one, as she scoured the beach from left to right and back again. Panic began to well up inside her. Where were they? At least they must all be together, and Mark was a sensible boy. Still the fears sent her heart thud, thud, thudding and her mouth felt dry and her legs as weak as jelly. It was true the tide was coming in, and coming in quite quickly now. Had they suddenly been cut off? Caught in a deep pool? No, it was impossible. The shore at this point was completely flat.

As she reached the water's edge, Mum suddenly spied four figures laughing and joking and wading towards her out of the sea. *Four* figures. Dad, Tim, Laura and Mark. She stood still, frozen to the spot, for a moment almost too paralysed to speak, and then she screamed out to them in a voice the children had never heard before — 'Theresa!' she shrieked. 'Where is she?'

# 9

## Lost

Mum stared at Mark's face. 'Where is she?' she demanded in amazement. 'Where *is* she?'

'She's gone back with Alice,' said Mark, frowning himself now and wondering why the two girls had not met his aunt. 'She got tired of waiting.'

'What!' exclaimed Mum with a mixture of anger and disbelief. 'You let two little girls wander off on their own on this huge, lonely beach! Mark, how could you?'

Mark gazed around at the wild emptiness and wondered himself how he could have done it. But at the time it had seemed like the best idea. Now fear began to grip him also.

As for Laura, she was speechless, utterly speechless. And when words finally came hissing forth, each one hit Mark like a bullet intended to kill.

'You – stupid – fool. You – lunatic. You – crazy – wicked – boy. You told us they'd gone with Mum! If they're lost,' her face twisted with pain, 'I'll never forgive you!'

Dad's face drained of colour and he stared vacantly at the acres of sand before them. Tim held his head in his hands and watched the waters steadily flowing inwards, each wave a few feet further up the beach. Laura looked to the right towards the mouth of the estuary, where the ground was anything but flat, and she remembered vividly how the tide swept in there, filling channels in moments, covering sandbanks in seconds.

It seemed like some terrible nightmare. But the facts were piercingly real.

'I'll go towards the river,' shouted Dad, setting off at a run. 'You children go to the right,' he called back over his shoulder, 'and Mum'll go to the left. Then meet up in the sand-dunes.'

Tim and Laura and Mark were already exhausted after their swim, and it was difficult to tell whether the numbness they felt was due to the cold water or this awful situation. All three forced themselves into action as the family fanned out silently to search for Theresa and Alice. Alice alone would have been bad enough, but at least she was fit and strong and a plucky child. But Theresa! It didn't bear thinking about.

All five of them combed the beach in every direction, seeing nothing but shells and seagulls, two boys shrimping and one man walking his dog.

As Laura, Tim and Mark neared the dunes, however, with no idea themselves where their original base might be, Mark noticed a white frilly object lying forlornly on the sand. It was Theresa's sunhat. Laura picked it up, tears blinding her eyes, and the three continued silently.

Once in the sandhills, it was impossible to know which way to turn. The ridges were so high, the dips so many, and even one large clump of grass could hide a whole family from view. Laura limped on with a feeling of dismal hopelessness. She'd hurt her foot on an unexpectedly rough stone. Here and there also were odd curls of rusty barbed wire, and the grass itself was tough and sharp on feet and fingers. Danger lurked everywhere.

The sun still shone, the sea still shimmered, but the beauty of the place had gone; its wonder changed to wildness, its freedom to fear. A train whistle sounded through the stillness, and the roar of its wheels caused Laura to shiver.

By luck more than anything else, the children stumbled on their belongings once more. Mum was already there, alone, peering around in great distress, and Dad soon panted into view, his face blank and his arms empty.

Suddenly, a cry was heard and everyone strained their ears to tell from what direction it was coming. Dad leapt to the top of a slope and looked around. There, stumbling towards him, overcome with the distance and the heat, was a weary and tear-stained Alice. He picked her up and carried her to the blanket.

'Where is she? Where's Theresa?' was all anybody could say.

Alice began to sob with relief at finding the family again, and it was some time before they could get any sense out of her. Finally, however, she admitted she had lost her sense of direction and ended up very near the dangerous currents. It was only the experience with her dad and Laura that first morning in the estuary that had warned her she must run for all she was worth to dry sand and safe ground. This she had done, carrying Theresa. Once she reached the sand-dunes, she had no idea where their own spot might be. She had stumbled on, exhausted, Theresa's clammy little arms round her neck. Finally her arms had given way and she had dropped the tired little girl on the soft sand. Theresa was so dazed with the heat and the glaring light that she immediately fell asleep. And Alice had left her there to go and search for help.

'Where?' demanded Laura, not unkindly, but with a dreadful urgency in her voice.

'I don't know,' moaned Alice. 'Over there somewhere . . .' She pointed vaguely across the waste of sand behind them.

'Look,' said Dad, 'we need help. We need help quickly, before Theresa wakes up and wanders down to the sea again, or hurts herself somewhere, or falls down a cliff or . . .'

'. . . before she gets sunstroke,' finished Mum solemnly.

'I daren't leave the beach,' Dad continued, 'in case, just in case she somehow turns up here. In fact I'll keep looking for her. Mum will stay here and you,' he turned to Tim and Mark, 'I want you two to go for help. That stone cottage, remember, over the golf-course, across the level crossing, and a few yards up the road? See if they have a telephone, and 'phone the police.'

'I'll go too,' said Laura, unable to stay still, despite her tiredness.

'And hurry,' urged Mum desperately, 'please hurry!'

How they ever reached the cottage, Laura couldn't quite remember, but reach it they did, and entered the strange semi-darkness after the glare of the mid-day sun. The quietly-spoken Welsh lady who lived there had seemed unwilling at first and suspicious, but Laura's pleadings eventually convinced her they were genuine. While Tim 'phoned the police, and Mark prompted him with details, Laura gulped back the choking feeling in her throat and wished there was something she could do to help. Anything just to keep her mind from the pathetic picture of Theresa, lost. A tiny helpless girl, not much more than a baby. And all alone.

As her eyes became used to the lack of light, Laura could make out details of the somewhat musty-smelling room in which they were standing. The furniture was dark and old-fashioned, high-backed chairs, embroidered cushions, a Welsh dresser full of fancy ornaments and plates, an old piano in which Laura would have been very interested on a happier occasion. There were old photographs all over the place, some in dulled silver frames, and there were pictures on every wall, dark gloomy pictures of misty hillsides, cows in a river, in frames of black or brown or ornate dusty gold. As she looked around, the largest painting of all caught Laura's attention. It was a full four feet in height and showed a child, a slim fair-haired girl, about to cross a dangerous narrow wooden plank over some rapids. To the front of the picture, beneath the bridge, was a chasm with dark swirling waters, whirlpools and jagged rocks. Behind the girl was an angel. Strong and real.

Laura gazed transfixed. Inside her something clicked into place. The something that might make all the difference to this awful day. She remembered that special verse her mum had given her for Theresa, printed over a modern day picture of a sleeping baby, instead of an old Victorian painting. But the message was the same, unchanged over the centuries:

'. . . these little ones . . . have their guardian angels in heaven, who look continually on the face of my heavenly Father.'

'Father,' prayed Laura silently. 'Send your guardian angels to watch over Theresa.' And she pictured the little girl, no longer alone, but sheltered by strong rustling wings.

Once the alarm had been sounded, action was very swift. As Laura, Mark and Tim made their weary way back to Mum and Dad, they heard and saw massive whirling helicopters overhead, and on the beach, speeding along the narrow strip of firm sand still left, was a land-rover with emergency equipment.

As soon as Theresa was spotted, still sound asleep on the sand, the land-rover drove as near as possible and two men rushed out carrying a blanket and a first-aid box. Dad was soon on the scene, followed by Mum, and the children watched, all near to tears, as the child was wrapped up and carried off to hospital, with Mum accompanying her.

'Will she be all right?' Laura whispered. It was a question she hardly dared ask.

'I think so,' said Dad quietly. 'She's not injured in any way but . . .' he hesitated and gave a deep sigh, 'she's been a heck of a long time in the sunshine.'

They packed up the bags silently, including the untouched picnic, and made their way back to the car. Dad drove the children home, left Tim in charge of them but under the care of the warden of the holiday village, and set off, without even stopping for a drink, to the hospital.

Tim and Mark and Alice nibbled half-heartedly at some bread rolls, but Laura wouldn't touch a thing. She sat in a deep arm-chair, hugging her knees and staring into space; and if her eyes did occasionally move, it was only to glare across at Mark with a silence that said guilty, guilty, guilty.

At last Mark could stand her accusing stare no longer. An idea had come to him, and it was for him the only way of surviving this ordeal. He emptied his money box of every single coin, checked in his pockets and rucksack, and set off down the hill to the village. If only he could buy Theresa that beautiful, expensive box of shells. Counting the money in his hand as he ran, he reckoned he had just about the required amount. It was the only way he could possibly say sorry. And he *was* sorry, sorry with all his heart. He knew Laura would never believe him, and probably neither would his aunt or uncle, but to make it up to Theresa, that was the important thing.

Mark was a strong, athletic boy, but the strain of the day was telling on him, and his eyes were somewhat glazed by the time he reached the shop. He stood still and tried to focus on the object he wanted, but all he could see was a blur of white and cream and pink and yellow as the hundreds of shell trinkets spread out before his eyes.

'The shell boxes?' he eventually asked the assistant. 'Where are they?'

'Sold out, son,' replied the man in charge. 'At least the little ones are. There are still a few larger ones. They're musical boxes too.' He adjusted his spectacles and picked up a large wooden box encrusted with shells and jewels and wound the key in the back. Notes as tinkling and delicate as the shells themselves floated around the shop.

'Good, isn't it?' he said with a smile.

'Yes,' agreed Mark, 'but how much does it cost?'

As he thought, it was much too expensive.

'The only other thing,' called the man, as Mark sadly made for the door, 'is to buy a little wooden box and a pack of shells and some glue and do it yourself!'

Mark's ears pricked up. Do it yourself! Yes, he was good with his hands, as with most other things, and it would certainly show how sorry he was if he spent hours making something for Theresa. It might not be as artistic as the ones in the shop, but he would have a really good try.

Mark chose a box, a tube of glue, some padding and a piece of pink satin. He was determined to do the job properly. He added the price up in his head, in order to calculate how much money was left for the shells. There was exactly seventy-five pence.

Seventy-five pence, would buy either one packet of small shells, or just one special exotic foreign shell. How Mark wished he could afford both! That beautiful shell would be ideal for the top of the box.

I know, thought Mark suddenly, I'll buy that one unusual shell, and I'll use my own shell collection for the rest! He even thought of borrowing his mum's pink pearl nail varnish, as he had seen Alice do many times, to brighten up some of the paler varieties. Already he was feeling much better.

'Thanks,' he smiled to the shopkeeper, and walked quickly up the hill, eager to start at once.

'What's in that bag?' asked Alice, as Mark returned.

'Nothing,' he replied, and tried to slip past her into his bedroom.

'Show me,' she snapped, 'or I'll tell Mum when she gets back.'

Anxious to avoid any more trouble, Mark opened the bag and took out the fancy foreign specimen. 'Just a shell,' he remarked.

Laura's ears pricked up as she watched curiously from her bedroom door across the passageway. She stood on tiptoe as Alice inspected the shell and gave it back to Mark.

'What d'you want that for?' Alice asked.

'Nothing,' he replied again.

Laura began to seethe in her normal fashion, and to

jump to conclusions as she usually did!

He's bought it for his shell collection, she thought to herself. Not content with losing Theresa, he's now going to cheat in the competition. How dare he? He's going to pretend he found that shell, and win first prize.

He doesn't care a bit about Theresa. He's too busy thinking about himself! Nasty, selfish, sly, pig-headed boy!

Mark worked quietly in his room all evening. Luckily Tim was out of the way watching television, and his parents were exhausted after their climb. Dad had come home with the good news that Theresa would be all right, but was being treated for sunstroke and exposure and would be kept in overnight for observation. Mum was staying with her. All being well, she would be allowed home the following afternoon.

The relief Mark felt over Theresa was enormous. It was as if a weight had been lifted from him, or a big dark cloud taken away. Thank goodness she's all right, he kept repeating to himself, as he worked and worked on her present. Thank goodness she's all right.

Now he could really enjoy making something for her. He tackled the inside first, and this was the hardest part as he had never worked with fancy materials before. The padding was a little lop-sided and the glue a bit smudgy, but the overall effect was pretty good.

Mark set the special large shell in place in the centre of the top of the box. It needed a lot of glue. The air in the bedroom was becoming quite full of its overpowering smell. Mark opened a window wide and let in the cool evening air. He could hear the wind in the pine trees and the rustling of the Russian vine against the window, and, in the distance, the gentle clink of the boats at their moorings near the harbour. Looking out for a moment's break, he noticed twinkling orange and green and gold lights. It was the village across the estuary. Stars sparkled in the sky, on this cool, clear evening, and all seemed well. The church clock chimed the hour and he set to work once more.

Mark spread out his whole collection of shells, the ones he'd spent hours naming and mounting for the competition, and he chose the very best for Theresa. The perfect unbroken ones, the most intricately designed and attractive, the most special and rare. Slowly the pattern grew and covered the top and sides. It was tedious, careful work, because each individual shell had to be held in position for a minute or more until the glue set. Patiently Mark worked on into the night, despite his tiredness, determined not to stop until he heard Tim's footsteps on the stairs. Then finally he placed the last minute, curly, shiny pink pyramid-shell into position, and held the box up to admire it in the light, giving a sigh of satisfaction and achievement.

Laura too felt a surge of relief run through her when she heard the news about Theresa.

'Thank you, God,' she whispered. 'Thank you for your holy angels.' But she still could not bring herself to forgive Mark. Especially now that he had cheated over the competition. And somehow she still felt miserable, even though Theresa would be home tomorrow. And somehow, despite the holy angels, God seemed very far away. How Laura wished she had a real friend to talk to!

As Dad and Pam and Barry were falling asleep in chairs, and as Alice was by now fast asleep in the top bunk, Laura decided she would finish off naming and displaying her shell collection. After all, Barry might realise Mark was cheating and disqualify him. She hoped so. Then she might win.

The next morning Barry was up bright and early. 'How are those fabulous collections?' he asked.

'Mine's finished,' replied Alice.

'And mine,' said Tim and Laura together.

'Yes, mine too,' added Mark. He knew he had no chance of winning now. He'd never be able to replace all the shells he had used.

'Go and get them,' said Barry. 'I'll judge them now as we're staying in this morning.'

Alice and Tim were soon back with boxes, and began to lay out their shells, Alice on the coffee table and Tim on a tray, with all their labels. Laura had hers already attractively mounted on sheets of plain paper, each shell named and also outlined in different coloured felt-tip pens. Tim had the most shells in number, but he had kept several of each variety.

'Where's Mark got to?' asked Barry, after he had examined each exhibit.

'Gone off to the village to buy some more shells,' muttered Laura to herself. She picked up Mark's football magazine as she was waiting, and amused herself by drawing beards and moustaches and long curly hair on all the players in his favourite team!

When Mark finally arrived, he had only one small sheet of card, and on it a few rather ordinary shells. She stared at him, puzzled, and expected him to draw out a brilliant display from behind his back any second, but he didn't.

'That all you've done?' questioned Barry in surprise. Mark nodded and didn't seem to care.

'Well,' announced Barry, 'there's no doubt about it – Laura is the winner!' He handed her a smooth and beautiful, pink and beige foreign shell, similar to the one

Mark had bought, but larger. 'Well done, Laura! A brilliant scientific display!'

Laura took the shell and said thank you, but her thoughts were far away. What on earth was Mark up to, she wondered? Some no-good sneaky plan, she was sure. What *had* he done with all his other shells? And where was that special one? She just *had* to know.

I'll hunt in his bedroom, she planned to herself, as soon as he and Tim go off to play table-tennis. I know Alice wants to go to the swings. I'll wait till Dad's busy in the kitchen, and Pam and Barry have gone shopping.

Laura knew it was wrong, but she did it all the same. Every drawer and cupboard she opened, searched in every corner, until there, on top of the wardrobe, was the answer. Laura climbed down from the chair holding the box of shells. Instantly the penny dropped. Theresa! He's made it for Theresa! Because of the box she liked in the shop. And he's done it all to take her away from me!

In her bitterness and rage, Laura felt like smashing the box to pieces there and then, crushing those delicate colours into a mass of shingle. Somehow, though, she couldn't bring herself to do it yet. She fingered the shiny shells, and the satin lining. It was beautiful, made with so much care and attention. She wondered for a moment whether she should take it and keep it for herself. Or should she stuff it in a village dustbin? Or throw it back in the sea?

For a moment even, she pictured the delight on Theresa's face and hesitated and almost put it back. Then she imagined the little girl hugging and kissing Mark and thanking him, and loving him all the more, and she hid the box under her sweater with new determination.

Whatever happened, Theresa was never going to see it.

# 10

## *Runaway*

'She's here!' shouted Tim, chasing up the steps to the car-park. Laura, Mark and Alice followed, almost tripping over each other in their eagerness. There was Mum, getting out of the car, with Theresa in her arms.

Laura held out her arms and Theresa willingly came to her. She seemed quieter than usual, a little bemused by it all, and when she did speak at last, it was to ask for Sammy Seagull.

Mark hesitated in the background. Would Theresa remember? Had she understood that it was all his fault? He wished he could give her the box on his own, without all the others watching. Someone had evidently bought her a new rag doll, which she clung to tightly.

While Barry and Pam were making tea for everyone, and Laura had actually left Theresa alone for a moment to go behind the kitchen hatch and practise a puppet show with Alice, Mark decided this was the right moment to present his gift. He reached up and slid his hand along the top of his wardrobe, but felt nothing but dust.

Frowning he fetched a chair and climbed up to have a good look. No, there was nothing there at all.

Mark stood still for a few seconds, poised on top of the chair. He couldn't understand it. He gazed round the room. Could Tim have moved the box? Surely not. He hunted under the beds, behind the curtains, in every drawer and cupboard, pulling out socks and shorts and T-shirts until the room looked as if it had been burgled. But there was still no sign of the box. As a last resort, he leant out from the open window and looked among the shrubs and bushes below.

Mark was shattered. Where else could it possibly be? Someone must have stolen it, though he couldn't imagine why. The worst thing was, he had already told Theresa he was going to fetch her a very special present. And her little face had lit up eagerly and the big brown eyes shone happily at him once more, convincing him that any ill-feeling between them was all forgiven and forgotten. Now he would have to disappoint her again. He looked around for something to take the place of the shell box, but he had nothing suitable. Finally he picked up his silver pen he'd won at school, and hurried upstairs with that.

'Ugh,' said Laura, 'what are you giving her that for? It's sharp. She could hurt herself on it.' She wrenched the pen from Theresa's hand. 'Mum, look, Mark's giving Theresa a dangerous pen!'

Theresa began to cry, because she liked the pen, but Laura picked her up and comforted her. 'Don't cry, darling. *We*'ve made a special welcome home puppet show for you! Come and sit on this chair.'

Theresa was soon laughing and calling out answers to the puppet characters which Laura and Alice skilfully handled. They weren't proper glove puppets, but a selection of toy animals, a dog, a rabbit, a bear and a cat, held up on the stage, together with all sorts of props from the kitchen. It was rabbit's birthday, and bear was making him a cake. Into the mixing bowl went a pack of butter, still wrapped, a carton of milk, an egg box plus eggs, still in their shells (here Mum caught Pam's eye and both heaved a sigh), some long spaghetti and plenty of salt and pepper. Mark had to admit that Laura was a real hit when performing for young children, and a comic into the bargain, judging by Theresa's shrieks of delight. He went off down to his bedroom again and stayed there alone until tea.

Laura was feeling decidedly pleased with herself, until her mum had a quiet word with her that evening.

'Laura, I want you to leave Mark alone,' she insisted. 'We've all forgiven him. In fact there wasn't much to forgive. If anyone was wrong really, it was me, for going off and leaving them in the first place. So I want *you* to forgive him, and everyone to be friends again, and end up this holiday happily.'

Laura opened and closed her mouth several times. She glared defiantly at her mother. 'No!' she exclaimed passionately, 'Not as long as I live!'

Her mother looked tired and weary and more than a little angry. 'Then you're a *very* unkind girl,' she said.

Laura stamped her foot, kicked the cupboards and made faces behind her mother's back as she turned to leave the room. So Mark had come out on top again! Goody, goody Mark, who couldn't do a thing wrong! She crawled right under the bottom bunk to where she had hidden the shell box in a brown paper bag. This was the moment to destroy it!

Furious as she was, however, Laura still could not actually bring herself to smash all those lovely shells. This made her all the more annoyed, annoyed with herself for being so soft. Still, she couldn't keep it in the bedroom much longer, in case Alice found it, so she stuffed it inside her sweatshirt, opened the door onto the patio and stepped out into the night.

It was not quite dark yet. The sky was sort of navy blue, with banks of clouds piling up behind the hillside. Laura hurried down the steps, along the paths, through the shrubbery until she reached their den. Perhaps there was somewhere she could hide the box, until the end of the holiday. She kicked around, looking for a dryish hole or space underneath a thick bush, but there was nowhere safe enough. She remembered the boys' cave, further up the hillside. If there was a cave among the rocks, surely there were holes and cracks around big enough to hide her secret.

Laura shivered slightly in the evening air. Darkness had suddenly fallen, and she wished she had a torch. Normally she would have been frightened to be outside in the trees alone, but her anger drove her to carry on with her plan.

She scrambled up the rocky, slippery path, brushing the brambles out of her hair, and scratching her hands and legs as she did so. Almost there. Then she turned to the left and the ground became grassy and soft with ferns. Laura stepped carefully and squeamishly on, dreading that she might step on some night creature, or fall down a hole.

At last, by the pale light of the moon as it appeared between the clouds, she found the cave, and felt for a large crack. Yes, there was one, near the entrance, which was just as well, as she dared not venture further. She folded the brown paper bag firmly round the box of shells and placed it down in the gap, feeling with her fingers to make sure it did not drop beyond reach.

'Done it!' she told herself proudly, and slid and slithered, sometimes on all fours, back down the steep path to the village.

Laura had no idea what time it was, but she hoped that Alice had not gone to bed yet. If so, she might have locked the bedroom patio door and Laura would then have to admit to her parents she'd been out alone.

Thankfully, she found the handle turned and the door opened easily, and there was no-one in the bedroom. There was a light in Mark's room though. She peeped through the slightly open door. He was pulling the beds out, moving all the pillows and covers, in a last desperate attempt to find the box.

Laura stopped in her tracks, feeling suddenly very guilty. Much as she hated Mark, there was something pathetic in the sight of him rummaging frantically amidst the bedclothes. She knew that what she had done was wrong. What if her parents ever found out? What if Mark told them and they questioned the whole family? It was all very well while no-one knew, but, if it came to the crunch, she was a rotten liar. Mum always guessed the truth just by one look at her reddening face.

And of course God knew the truth already. He *would*, wouldn't he? And he would be bound to be on Mark's side.

Laura felt miserable and wretched, but utterly sorry for herself and determined not to give in.

'I'll give them all a scare,' she mumbled. 'I'll run away for the whole night! Perhaps that will take their minds off Mark and his stupid box.'

Laura retraced her steps through the bedroom, picked up her anorak and torch and once more opened the door into the night. Swiftly she made her way down the steps, along the path, down some more steps and out onto the road. Then she took the lane, which was a steep short-cut, past the pottery shop and the art gallery, down to the road by the estuary.

Everything seemed different at night, and at first Laura wondered whether she had taken a wrong turn. No, there was the harbour, far on her right, the pinky-orange street lights glowing, the lighted shop and cottage windows also marking out the way.

Laura stepped onto the sand and sat on an upturned boat. There was no-one else to be seen by the sea, though the two hotels and a pub on the other side of the road were overflowing with yacht-owners and holidaymakers.

She thought she was alone until a large shadowy shape, wolf-like in appearance Laura thought, came silently towards her. She froze while the animal sniffed around her feet and then continued on its way.

The next thing that she noticed was that the waves were lapping close beside her. Better go to the shelter by the yacht club, she decided. Safer there.

The seat was certainly dry and the concrete firm beneath her feet, but it was cold in there and very dark, facing away from the village and out towards the sea. A figure shuffled by, an elderly man in a raincoat as far as she could tell. She held her breath for a few moments, hoping upon hope that he would not decide to sit down and join her. Then there was a whirring, dragging sound from somewhere along the promenade. What on earth could it be? Laura slunk further into the corner, and wished she was invisible. If she hadn't been so scared, she might have shone her torch to investigate, but the last thing she wanted to do was to draw attention to herself.

The church clock struck ten, its chimes pealing out across the bay. Laura snuggled deeper into the collar of her anorak, and tapped her icy feet on the ground. It was going to be a long night.

A cluster of crab pots stood just in front of her, together with a few marker buoys. Laura remembered with awful clearness the giant crab she had found on Shell Island. She remembered too the spooky tale Uncle Barry had told.

Try as she might she couldn't think of anything pleasant. She looked back towards the estuary – deep swirling waters. She looked down into the harbour – black murky depths. The dogfish, with its sharp fin, came into her mind; the dense, dark forest; the full horror of Theresa's scare. She remembered the cottage, the gloomy pictures – and then, finally, the angel! Did she have a guardian angel looking after her?

Laura wanted to cry out to God, but she felt he was nowhere near at all. It was like those mountains, solid, clear and sharp one moment in the sunshine, then vanished in clouds and mist the next. One day God was there, the next he was far away. It was no good, he wasn't even listening.

The spider was the final straw. As Laura leant her head back further into the corner to rest, she felt a tickling sticky mass of threads catching her hair and ear, and then, horror of horrors, a spider dropped right into her neck!

'Aah!' she screamed out loud, but there was no-one to hear. 'Please, God,' she cried out, 'you've got to help me! Where are you?'

In her desperation, Laura forced herself to reason more clearly. You can't always see the tops of the mountains, Barry had said, but they're always there. You can't always feel God with you, she remembered hearing at church one day, but he is always there. It's just that clouds have got in the way. With them hanging over us, we don't feel God is there at all. But he *is* there all the time, and he *does* still care. When we clear the clouds away, we can feel him close once more.

But how to clear the clouds away, that was the problem. She thought over all the things she'd done to hurt Mark. Must she be punished?

In the silence and the stillness, out of nowhere it seemed, came the words of an old hymn:

What a friend we have in Jesus,
All our sins and griefs to bear!

Laura remembered and felt more intensely than ever her own need and prayer for a friend. She also remembered that Jesus had already taken her punishment for her, dying on the cross to take away all her sins.

'Lord Jesus, please forgive me,' she whispered in the darkness. 'I'm so sorry for everything I've done. Please be my friend.'

Then Laura knew that God was with her after all; and the angels were protecting her. She left the cold cheerless shelter and set off up the hill once more. The first thing she had to do was get the box – tomorrow if possible – and put it back in Mark's room. Then she would have to tell him she was sorry for all the things she'd said.

Laura climbed the steps quickly, in the eerie light of an old lamp post. Bushes and branches, strange shapes and shadows, ghostly flowers brushed against her legs and face on the overgrown path.

Shining comfortingly ahead of her was the large lighted window of their lounge. Laura could see her mum and dad, Pam, Barry and Tim, all playing a game round the coffee table. It amazed her that they weren't all looking out for her. Obviously they hadn't even realised she was missing.

Laura reached the patio and tried the bedroom door. 'Oh, no!' It was firmly locked. She rattled the handle, trying to wake Alice, but it was no good. Laura walked round the house looking for an open window, but there was none large enough. Finally she noticed a light and looked through the open curtains into Mark's room.

There he was, not reading or playing, or getting ready for bed, but kneeling beside the chair. Laura bit her lip and moved back behind the wall again. She hadn't realised Mark believed in God. She never would have guessed he'd be the kind of boy to pray. And she didn't have to think very hard to realise what he was praying about.

Laura waited until Mark got up from his knees, and then gave a gentle tap on the window. Mark looked up in amazement, and opened it to let her climb in. They stared at each other, lost for words, but, in a sense, not needing any. Their eyes met, Laura's very misty, and she told him sincerely, 'Mark, I'm sorry.'

There was no time for any more explanations, because Mum came in, having heard the noise. She was surprised to find Laura there, thinking she had gone to bed with Alice.

'Time for lights out,' she said, and Laura made for the door. Her mum put an arm round her, as if sensing that apologies had been made and all was well once more. 'Goodnight, both of you,' she said. 'God bless.'

# 11

## *The shell box*

For once Laura awoke later than all the others and the first thing which came to mind was a plan to be left on her own to get back the box.

Ignoring the breakfast table, where the others were just finishing their toast, Laura flopped down on an armchair with a heavy sigh. She was a born actress.

'Oooh!' she moaned. 'My head! I'll have to stay at home on my own this morning for a rest.'

'But we're going to the beach!' said Alice in concern. 'All of us this time, and you won't want to miss it. My mum and dad are coming in the sea with us too.'

Laura looked out across the balcony to the cool smooth, refreshing sea. High tide it was and utterly calm this morning, greeny-blue glassy water, with sunshine highlighting the little boats, white, blue, red, green and brown with their orange marker buoys. She p~~ ~~ herself kicking and splashing and swimming ~~ ~~ along the coast in the clear unruffled wat~~ ~~ pictured the shell box, in the brown p~~ ~~

crack in the rocks on the hillside. Swimming would have to wait. She had to get the box back first.

'We can't leave you all on your own,' said Mum sympathetically. 'We'll find a place where the road is nearer the beach, so you don't have to walk so far, and we'll take the big sunshade.'

Laura thought quickly. Despite all her efforts, it seemed that her headache had not been bad enough. 'Ooh,' she groaned, shading her eyes with her hand. 'Could somebody close the curtains please? Oooh! The pain! I think I'll have to go to bed!'

Mum helped her downstairs again and she collapsed onto the bottom bunk, having no strength to climb to the top one. 'I'll soon be all right, Mum,' she whispered nobly. 'Just one of my headaches, that's all!'

'Well, dear, if you're sure you don't mind us leaving you?' Mum tucked her up. 'We'll be back for lunchtime and perhaps you'll feel like coming out this afternoon.'

Great, thought Laura with a sigh of relief. I'll get the box back this morning and be free to go out this afternoon. She heard the front door slam shut. Her plan had worked! Alone at last.

'I don't want to disturb you, dear,' whispered Pam, peeping round the bedroom door, 'but just try one of these tablets. They're really good, always get rid of my headaches.'

Laura looked up in dismay.

'I said I'd stay, dear. It's not nice being on your own when you don't feel well.'

Laura took the glass of water offered her, and looked at the huge white pill. 'I'll have it later, thank you,' she said.

'No, have it now, so it works by this afternoon,' insisted Pam, taking the tablet and breaking it into four pieces.

'One at a time,' she said firmly, 'makes it easier to swallow!'

Laura gulped down some water and placed a piece of tablet in the corner of her mouth. She was intending to spit it out later. The taste was so horrible, however, she was forced to swallow it – and the other three quarters!

Now what do I do, she thought. She looked over to the patio door. Well, she would just have to slip out without Pam knowing. At least the other children weren't around to follow her and ask awkward questions.

All would have gone smoothly, had Pam not decided to sunbathe on the balcony. Just as she was about to settle herself on a sunbed, she noticed Laura's red T-shirt speeding furtively along the path below.

'Laura, where on earth are you going?' she called in bewilderment.

'Marvellous tablets!' called back Laura over her shoulder. 'Better already! Just need some fresh air!'

Pam gave a sigh and closed her eyes in the sunshine. These children! One minute they were in agony, the next completely recovered! It was hard to keep track of them!

When Laura reached the cave, however, she was in for a nasty shock. There just ahead of her were three other children, two teenage girls, it seemed, and a boy of about Tim's age.

'Golly gosh,' said the boy, 'I say, there's a cave in the rocks.'

'Gosh,' echoed the girls, 'so there is!'

'Don't go inside, Toby,' warned the taller girl. 'You might get mud on your trousers.'

'Look here,' said the second girl, her hand down the crack where Laura had hidden the box. 'I say, someone's hidden something!'

'Don't touch it,' ordered the first girl, with her nose in

the air. 'Oh, how filthy!' she continued, as her sister drew out the now damp, torn and dirty paper bag.

'Leave it alone, Amelia. It's covered in germs! Throw it away!'

Laura watched stunned, as the children hesitated with her precious brown paper bag. The elder girl snatched it and was about to hurl it down the hillside, when Toby grabbed it from her.

'Hold on, Polly-Anna,' he scolded. 'There might be something valuable inside.' He unwrapped the soggy remains of the paper, and there, as good as new, was Mark's beautiful box, each and every tiny shell intact.

'I say, how splendid!' gasped Polly-Anna.

'What a find!' agreed Amelia. 'Let's go and show Mummy.'

'Yah,' nodded Polly-Anna, 'and we must wash our hands.'

The children had not even noticed Laura, and were about to depart down the hill. If she let them go now, the box would be lost for ever, and she had no idea where they might be staying. Taking a deep breath, and summoning all the courage she ever possessed for they were all bigger than her, Laura called out, 'Hey, you lot, that box belongs to me!'

The oldest, Polly-Anna, turned to stare at Laura. 'I beg your pardon?' she said, with a toss of her long straight hair.

'The box,' repeated Laura, 'I hid it there last night. I was just coming to get it. It's mine.'

Polly-Anna looked at Amelia, and Amelia looked at Toby. Clearly they did not believe a word Laura said.

'So you made it, did you?' asked Amelia, with a sarcastic glare.

'N-no,' faltered Laura, 'my cousin made it.'

'And does your cousin know you hid it?' demanded Toby.

'No,' murmured Laura.

'And where is this famous cousin of yours?' asked Polly-Anna.

'Gone to the beach,' said Laura honestly.

'So he can't be very concerned about the box!' concluded Polly-Anna. And the three of them set off down the hillside.

'But you're stealing it!' Laura called after them in desperation. She wished Tim were with her now. He would know what to do.

'You prove your cousin exists,' shouted Polly-Anna, 'and we'll give him his box.'

Laura followed the children back to the hillside village, hoping against hope that they were holidaying there, and she might find out where they were staying. She knew that if they were living further away, all would be lost.

Keeping a safe distance behind them, dodging behind bushes and shrubs here and there for cover, Laura at last saw them enter the front door of a house very similar to their own, and only a few paths away. At least she knew where the box was, though how to get it back she couldn't imagine.

Wearily Laura made for her room. She would have to think this out before Mark got back. Dare she knock on the door and demand the box once more? What would the children's parents be like? The awful thing was, she had no proof the box was hers, for no-one else in her family even knew of its existence. That is, apart from Mark!

Blow those snooty children! What were their names? Toby, Amelia and . . . Polly . . . er . . . Polly-Anna . . . who thought she was so clever. 'Polyunsaturates' Laura would call her.

'Mark,' whispered Laura, after lunch. 'Could you come and speak to me in private for a moment?'

Mark left the jigsaw he was starting and followed Laura outside onto the pathway.

'Mark,' she hesitated, not knowing really how to begin to explain, 'Mark, you know that box you made, and it got lost? Well, I'm sorry, but it was me! I took it.'

Mark stared at her in astonishment. 'But why?' he said.

Laura shrugged her shoulders uncomfortably, 'Because I was jealous, I suppose. I don't like it when Theresa prefers you. I'm sorry.'

Understanding came into Mark's eyes, and a sudden joy that all his work was not wasted. He would be able to give Theresa the box after all.

'Where is it, then?' he asked. 'Can I have it back now?'

'Well,' mumbled Laura awkwardly, 'you see, I hid it, and now some stupid children have stolen it.'

'Where do they live?' asked Mark. 'I'll go and get it back.'

'They said they would give it back if *you* came,' continued Laura encouragingly. As long as Mark knocked on the door and not her!

They made their way towards the children's holiday house, and there was the box proudly displayed on a bedroom window sill. The small top window was open.

'Shall I climb up and get it?' suggested Laura. 'If I put my hand through that little window, I might just be able to reach the handle of the big window.'

'No,' said Mark firmly, 'that would be stealing.'

'But they stole it first,' protested Laura.

'And *you* stole it in the first place,' added Mark sharply, 'otherwise none of this would have happened. There's been too much stealing going on!'

110

Laura was silent. She knew he was right. He had seemed to forgive her, but he would still be upset and angry until they got the box back.

They reached the front door and Laura plucked up courage and knocked. Polly-Anna opened it, and seemed a little taken aback to find the two of them there.

'Here's my cousin,' said Laura, simply and politely. 'We want the box back please.'

'How do we know you're not lying?' said Polly-Anna. 'We won't give you the box unless your parents come to back up your story.'

Mark looked disappointed and ready to give up. 'They don't even know I made it,' he said quietly. 'We've no proof at all.'

Polly-Anna slammed the door.

Laura stood on the step fuming. 'They're *not* getting away with it,' she muttered, pushing her hair behind her ears in a determined fashion. Mark had already walked away.

With a boldness she never knew she possessed, Laura banged on the door once more. 'Please, Lord,' she whispered under her breath, 'please make them give it back.'

This time Toby and Amelia opened the front door.

'I've shown you my cousin, and now I want the box, please,' insisted Laura. 'It's *wrong* to keep something that doesn't belong to you. And,' she glared defiantly at them, hands on hips, 'I'm *not* going away until you give me it!'

Just then an old green Jaguar drew into the parking place and the children's parents got out.

Amelia turned red, and Toby hurried off to get the box. 'Here you are!' he said and thrust the box into Laura's outstretched hand. 'Now perhaps you'll be satisfied.'

It was hard to tell whether Mark or Laura was the more relieved to see Theresa with her present at last. Her big brown eyes opened wide in amazement, as if she could hardly believe something so special was actually for her. She opened the lid and felt the satin; she pointed to the decoration and kept repeating, 'S'ells! T'resa's s'ells, no lady's s'ells, T'resa's s'ells!' Then 'Box! T'resa's box, no lady's box, T'resa's box!' Finally, still clutching her box, she clambered up on to Mark's lap and gave him a big hug and a kiss.

Surprisingly enough, Laura found she was no longer jealous. 'Come and show Laura,' she said to Theresa, and the little girl climbed down from Mark and walked over to sit beside her on the floor by the window.

'Aren't you lucky?' said Laura. 'Mark made that specially for you, you know. He used up all his best shells. You'll have to be very careful with it. Then when you're a big girl, you can use it for a jewellery box. Put all your pretty rings in it!'

It was difficult to persuade Theresa to leave the box behind, when the families went down to the beach again that afternoon. But Laura placed it in her cot, beside all her animals, and reassured her it would be quite safe.

This time everyone went into the sea in swimsuits, even Theresa. Laura was glad to see the little girl seemed to have forgotten her frightening experience, and had a wonderful time jumping over the ripples, lying down and kicking her legs and splashing and shouting: 'T'resa 'wimmin', T'resa 'wimmin'!'

Dad had bought her a fishing net too, and Alice managed to catch three tiny shrimps for her which she kept proudly in her bucket all afternoon. Then Laura found her a baby starfish, and Tim added a spider crab to the collection.

112

Finally both families enjoyed a tea-time picnic in the shelter of the dunes. The air was warm, the breeze gentle, swaying through the tall green grasses. For once everyone was on good terms with everyone else, and it seemed that the heartache of just two days ago had completely vanished.

# 12

## On top of a mountain

'Oh, Mum,' moaned Laura in disapproval, 'you're *not* going to wear that ridiculous hat?'

Mum looked in the bedroom mirror at the large floppy pink sunhat on her head. 'What's wrong with it?' she asked. 'Dad bought it for me.'

'It's . . . it's . . . *ludicrous*!' exploded Laura.

Just at that moment a family passed by the window on their way down to the beach.

'Look,' shouted Laura, 'that settles it! Polyunsaturates' mother is wearing one too! That proves it's awful!'

'Polly who?' questioned Mum.

'Oh, Polly-Anna really,' admitted Laura. 'We've met them around the village. They're so posh, think they're better than anyone else!'

'What a shame,' said Mum. 'Would have been nice for you to meet some new friends.'

'Anyway,' said Laura, returning to the subject of hats, 'I'm *not* going out with you wearing that!'

'Luckily you don't have to,' replied Mum. 'Barry has

suggested taking you and Tim and Mark to climb a mountain today, as the weather's suitable. It's your last chance before we go home tomorrow.'

'What are the rest of you doing?' asked Laura.

'We're taking Theresa for a last day on the beach.'

'Oh,' said Laura, 'I don't really want to leave her . . . but, on the other hand, we'll soon be back to flat old home, and I won't even see another mountain for a whole year.'

'Yes,' agreed Mum, 'and you'll have Theresa all day on the journey tomorrow.'

Pam came round the door waving a pair of heavy walking boots in one hand and some thick socks in the other. 'Try these for size, Laura,' she said. 'Should be all right with two pairs of socks.'

'Good thing the girls at school can't see me,' sighed Laura, as she tied the laces. 'Football boots are one thing, but these . . . well . . .'

Finding they fitted, Laura then sorted out a warm jumper and her cagoule, and made sure she had some sweets in the pockets. Best be prepared on one of their expeditions, she thought to herself.

She kissed Theresa goodbye, promised Alice she'd bring her some rock from the top, and off they went.

Barry stopped the car in a neat little car-park beside a quiet ivy-covered restaurant. Apparently the climb started from this point, and the first part of the track passed a series of popular waterfalls in a wooded valley. Certainly there were several other walkers around.

'Why aren't they wearing climbing boots?' complained Laura. 'Thought you said we *had* to?'

'They're not tackling the tough stuff!' explained Barry. 'So stop fussing, Laura! Anyway, the boots suit you!'

Tim, Mark and Laura strode on ahead, eager to see

what was round each corner. The first waterfall was high but narrow, a single silver stream dropping down, down, down over a sheer rock face. At the side were bright green ferns and foxgloves, pockets of moss and leaves shining in the sunshine. Laura couldn't help noticing all the different shades of green. It was beautiful.

As they climbed higher, there were steps hewn into the rock, or wooden ones, to help them up the slippery path. Sometimes tree roots formed a sort of staircase. Sometimes the children had to cling to overhanging branches to help them over a muddy patch. And some-times, due to heavy rainfall the previous night, the path itself turned into a stream, and logs were used as stepping stones.

The second waterfall was less high than the first, but fanned out over a wider rock surface. Laura marvelled at how white it was, cascading into the pool below. There the main colour was brown – the pebbles, the rocks, the mud, the whirling water itself, all different shades of brown.

By the time they reached the third waterfall, Laura felt a definite ache behind her knees, but it was well worth it. They had climbed right out of the woods and onto the open hillside.

'Look at this one,' gasped Mark, as he clambered over jagged rocks towards the pounding spray. This time it was possible to reach the very foot of the fall, and feel the misty dampness on your face and swish your fingers through one of the icy pools below. Laura picked up some coloured pebbles and put them in her pocket to remind her of the place.

'Now,' said Barry, shielding his eyes and gazing up at the mountain slopes above them. 'This is the part I'm not sure about. I can't *see* any path up this mountain, but I'm certain there must be one, and we can't possibly get lost because all we have to do is keep climbing the waterfalls!'

Laura looked up at the little white ribbon of a stream wiggling its way down the hillside.

'Is *that* where we're going?' she gasped.

'That's it!' replied Barry. 'Right up to find the source of the stream. The map shows a lake. Then on to the top of the mountain!'

'If we don't get lost first,' added Tim. 'Or fall down a precipice, or sink in a swamp!'

They climbed a rough grey wall, and walked through a stone sheep pen. Several nervous sheep stood up hurriedly, rising first on their back legs, and followed one another out of the opening. More were nibbling grass outside, and these too scuttled away.

From then on the ground rose extremely steeply, in places almost vertically, ahead of them. The grass was springy and tufty in places and long in others. The clumps were good for holding onto as they heaved themselves up the hillside. Barry had been wrong! There was certainly no path!

As they climbed higher and higher, the view became more and more spectacular. Mountain upon mountain, in all their sunny splendour.

No-one had much breath for talking, but all did plenty of thinking. It was good to be up so high, away from the noise and dirt and hustle and bustle of everyday life. It was good to be alone, to have space to breathe. It was impossible, or at least so Laura thought, to be in the middle of so much beauty without thinking about the greatness of the God who made it all. If she'd been completely alone, she'd have shouted out thank you, thank you, thank you, till it echoed and resounded round the hillsides. As it was, she whispered thank you in her heart.

'Only one more hill and we've reached the top of the stream,' shouted Tim suddenly.

Sure enough there they were on marshy boggy ground covered with white fluffy bog cotton, on a level with the very highest point of all the waterfalls. It was splendid. The lake, however, was more like a swamp and it was almost impossible to find the edges to walk around it, as every patch of grass was squelching with water.

'Now you see why you need strong boots!' remarked Barry, as he lifted up one soaking wet foot. 'You all right, Laura!'

Somehow they manoeuvred their way round the edge of the field and began to climb the now rocky path to the summit. The wind was strong, despite the lovely sunny day, and it was hard to keep their balance. Mark held out his hand to help Laura two or three times, and she realised happily just how fond she was of her cousin, now the jealousy had gone.

'Well done!' he said to her in admiration as they climbed up the final sloping stretch of sheer rock. 'This is the hardest climb I've *ever* done, and it's your first!' Laura glowed with pride.

'Yes,' agreed Barry, his curly hair blowing all over his face, 'well done, Laura. It's hard enough climbing with a path, and today we've climbed without one. Exciting, wasn't it?'

'Yes,' agreed Laura breathlessly, as she bent down and picked up a small piece of rock for Alice.

'Mad, if you ask me!' called out Tim, as he placed a larger rock on the windy cairn on the summit. 'But there must have been other mad people here before us!'

'What worries me,' admitted Barry honestly, 'is the

way down. It was so steep in places – we'll have to slide down on our bottoms' (Laura looked with regret at her new blue jeans) 'and it won't be at all easy. Unless,' he added, drawing a map out of his pocket, 'I can find another way.'

'Here we go,' sighed Mark, 'couldn't possibly follow the same way back – much too boring! Can we at least have our food first?'

They clambered down to the shelter of a big rock, and ate the picnic Mum had prepared. Laura smiled as she pictured Mum in her awful pink sunhat on the beach. Perhaps she would meet up with Polly-Anna's mum. Bet those three could never climb a mountain, she thought. In fact I don't know why I was ever afraid of them.

It was doing things for Laura, this holiday. Making her realise she was much stronger and bolder than ever she thought. When I get back to school, she pondered, things are going to be different. I'm going to stand up for myself! I'm going to say what *I* think's right, whether the others are likely to agree or not! Funny place to make such an important decision, huddled here on a bleak and blowy mountain. But perhaps clear mountain tops are places where decisions can be made.

The way down was just as exciting as the way up! In fact, as the party descended a different wooded valley, much wilder than the first, it became clear that the most awesome waterfalls were still to be discovered.

The first came crashing, roaring, thundering, foaming down about sixty feet to a bubbling cauldron below. The spray soaked them like fine rain. There was something tremendous, yet awful, beautiful and breath-taking, yet terrifying about its power and the black jagged rocks and endless whirlpools. It was grand, but solemn. There were two straight fallen pines across the rocks, completely stripped of leaves, bark, branches. Laura was glad to leave it behind. You couldn't relax there. One careless step and . . . It didn't bear thinking about.

Far below that the main falls spread out like an open white lace fan. The cascades were decorating the hillside with their foaming curves and patterns, and the rocks were light and friendly enough to allow little silver birches to grow right on the edge of the water.

'Glad you came?' asked Barry, his arm round Laura's shoulder.

'Tremendous!' whispered Laura. 'I've never seen anything more beautiful in my whole life!'

When they all finally reached the road once more, Barry reckoned that the car was parked about two miles away, and all three children were utterly exhausted. Just as he was debating what best to do, Tim noticed a tea-garden by a river, by a thatched cottage. So the three of them waited there licking ice-creams (Tim had two!) sipping lemonade and enjoying the peace of the place. There was a stone bridge over the river, and wooden picnic benches. There were hens pecking around, three white ducks, a dog and some sheep. It was quiet and green and gentle, the perfect end to a perfect outing.

Laura did think of tricking Barry by all hiding beneath the bridge when he came back to fetch them. To pay him back for the 'crab' story. But all three were too tired to make the effort.

Back at the village by late afternoon, however, after a welcome rest in the car, the children's strength had amazingly returned. So when Alice ran to meet them and asked them for a last game of table-tennis, Mark, Tim and Laura readily agreed.

When they reached the sports room, however, they found that Polly-Anna and family were attempting to play. The ball rarely hit the table, and if it did they usually missed it.

'We could thrash them,' whispered Mark wickedly.

'Yes,' grinned Laura, 'come on!'

'Hi, Polly-Anna,' she bounced over confidently. 'How about a challenge? Me 'n' my cousin Mark, against you or Amelia and Toby?'

Polly-Anna and company felt decidedly awkward, but Laura looked as if she would not take no for an answer.

The match began, with Alice scoring. One nil, two nil, three nil, four nil . . . Twenty-one nil! Game! In fact it was hardly a match at all, with Mark and Laura winning every point!

Toby held out his hand to Mark. 'Well played,' he admitted. 'I'm useless at table-tennis. Haven't had any practice.'

Polly-Anna and Amelia could not hide their admiration of Laura. Clearly there was more to this girl than met the eye.

'We're sorry about the box,' said Amelia at last. 'It was just that we didn't believe you at first.'

Laura gasped in amazement. These two toffee-nosed teenagers actually apologising to her! She almost collapsed with shock!

'Oh, that's all right,' she answered casually. 'Have you had a good holiday?'

'First rate,' replied Toby.

'Yes, enormous fun,' agreed the other two.

'Well,' said Laura,' we'd better go now. Dinner will be ready. See you in the morning perhaps. Bye!'

It was sad yet satisfying for all the children to have a last night walk up the steep hill from the village, past the lit-up cottages, with their small rooms and open stairs and old-fashioned fireplaces and uneven walls.

The dark steps and shadowy flowers reminded Laura of the night she ran away. It was much better to be with the family, holding Mum and Dad's hands, than to be alone. Much better now that she was holding God's hand too, thought Laura. One day she would tell her mother all that had happened.

The end of the holiday had come at last, and no-one, least of all Laura, wanted to go home. Still, the packing had to be done, and she struggled sadly with the T-shirts and sweaters which would keep spilling out of her case, no matter how hard she rammed them in.

Theresa appeared at the bedroom door – she had slept late and was still in her white nightie. Barefooted, she had teddy under one arm and rabbit under the other, and her big brown eyes were still dazed and not quite awake. Laura held out her arms and the little one toddled in. Her cheeks were soft and smooth and beautifully tanned a shade darker than normal. Her bare arms were chubby and warm. Laura held her silently, and felt a lump coming in her throat. She hadn't dared ask Mum and Dad much about it, but she feared the end of the holiday would mean goodbye to Theresa.

All too soon the cars were loaded and the children took a last longing look from the balcony out over the estuary and the mountains beyond, the view that had been theirs for two whole weeks. Now it was good-bye to all that, good-bye to each other, and a final farewell wave to Sammy Seagull as he strutted along the rooftop.

Mark and Alice leant out of the car window and waved back madly to their cousins before Barry sped on up the coast road out of sight. I'll miss Alice, thought Laura to herself; and then her eyes fixed on the shell box held tightly in Theresa's hands. And I'll actually miss Mark.

Why do holidays speed by in a few seconds, but journeys take a hundred years? I wish it had all been a dream and we would wake up and start all over again!

With several sighs Tim and Laura watched the rugged mountain scenery give way to rolling hillsides, and these in turn flatten out to uninteresting fields on the edge of the motorway. No-one spoke much, Theresa nodded off to sleep; and finally there they were back in their own driveway looking out at the uncut lawn and the overgrown flower borders.

Dad will be out there working hard tomorrow morning, thought Laura. Then he'll clean the car, hose down the driveway and read the Sunday papers. Why, oh why, couldn't he come to church with us? Even just once?

'We're going to sing to God and Jesus,' explained Laura to Theresa the next morning. 'Nice singing, lah, lah, lah. Theresa sing? Theresa sing Jesus loves me?' She brushed the dark curls, balancing the little girl skilfully on one knee, despite her bouncing about. 'Pity this'll be the last as well as the first time Theresa comes with us,' she murmured to her mother.

Mum looked at Laura knowingly. 'It won't be the last,' she said. 'In fact it'll be the first of many. It's true Theresa's mum is taking her back very soon, now she's out of hospital, but they still want us to help by having her for weekends and holidays. They think it will be good for them both.'

Laura's arms tightened around Theresa, and she felt she was the luckiest person in the world.

Just then Dad called from the bedroom, 'Where's my shirt?' Laura looked up questioningly at her mother, as if she could hardly believe her ears.

'Yes,' whispered Mum, 'he's coming, but *don't* make any comments and *don't* expect it to last! I think it had something to do with Theresa's accident on holiday. I'm not sure. Perhaps he made a promise to come if she got better. People do strange things like that when they're in a panic.'

Yes, thought Laura sympathetically, remembering her dark evening by the sea. People do pray in panics.

She thought back over all her promises this summer. Promises easily made, and just as easily forgotten. Her last promise had not been easily made, however, and nor, with God's help, would it be broken. From now on she was really trying to follow Jesus.

She'd asked for a lot of things this summer too. And her prayers had been answered, if not always in the way she had expected. She remembered once again the prayer for a friend back at school. She was sure it would be answered too, though she no longer expected a perfect companion to drop from the skies as it were, on the first day of term. Now Laura had found her best friend in Jesus, she was strong enough to believe she would find a friend in class too. Perhaps some of those quieter, shy girls were really worth getting to know. Or perhaps some of the 'harder' set could be softened up a bit if she said what she thought and encouraged them to be nice. After all, she thought, even Polly-Anna was friendly in the end! And as for me, well, I'm not perfect!

So it was a confident Laura who set off for school some three weeks later, with a new grey straight skirt, white open-necked blouse and a black shoulder bag swinging casually from her left arm. And it was a happy and surprisingly forceful Laura who burst through the classroom door, determined to hold her own from now on.

'Hi, every one!' she shouted. 'How was the holiday? *We* had a great time. I went with my cousin Mark. He's

125

terrific! Looks a bit like a pop-star! You should see him play football! He taught me how to dive for the ball! And we went rock-climbing! And we took this little girl with us. She's really sweet! And Mark made this fantastic shell box!

'And when's five-a-side football practice going to start?'